THE DREADFUL DEBUTANTE

THE DREADFUL DEBUTANTE

Marion Chesney

Chivers Press • G.K. Hall & Co.
Bath, England   Thorndike, Maine USA

This Large Print edition is published by Chivers Press, England, and by G.K. Hall & Co., USA.

Published in 1999 in the U.K. by arrangement with Robert Hale Ltd.

Published in 1999 in the U.S. by arrangement with Barbara Lowenstein Associates.

U.K. Hardcover   ISBN 0–7540–3631–6 (Chivers Large Print)
U.K. Softcover   ISBN 0–7540–3632–4 (Camden Large Print)
U.S. Softcover   ISBN 0–7838–8502–4 (Nightingale Series Edition)

The text of this Large Print edition is unabridged.
Other aspects of the book may vary from the original edition.

Set in 16 pt. New Times Roman.

Printed in Great Britain on acid-free paper.

British Library Cataloguing in Publication Data available

Library of Congress Cataloging-in-Publication Data

Chesney, Marion.
    The dreadful debutante / Marion Chesney.
    p. (large print) cm.
    ISBN 0–7838–8502–4 (lg. print : sc : alk. paper)
    1. Large type books.   I. Title.
    [PR6053.H4535D74   1999]
    823'.914—dc21   98–32201

For Annette Clayton

CHAPTER ONE

Never had two sisters so close in age looked so little alike. Drusilla Markham was very beautiful, tall, statuesque, elegant, a perfect Regency beauty—with liquid dark eyes, thick brown hair, and a figure that had that necessary rounded look for beauty. Her sister, Mira, short for Mirabelle, was small with dark, wiry hair, large green eyes, and unfashionably high cheekbones in an age when women plumped out their cheeks with wax pads to achieve the desired Dutch doll effect.

Where Drusilla was calm and gracious, Mira was fiery, tetchy, and restless.

Like most children of aristocrats they had been brought up by a nurse and then a governess, rarely seeing their parents. The trouble started early on. Drusilla had always been beautiful, but Mira had heard herself described at an early age as a 'changeling'. The nurse doted on Drusilla and paid scant attention to Mira. The governess followed the same pattern, being the sort of governess who considered proper education harmful to young misses, and so it was Drusilla who could play the harp gracefully, embroider well, and who received all the praise.

Mira adored her father. Mr. Markham, of the untitled aristocracy, was a cold, withdrawn man, but Mira had once heard him say he longed for a son, and so she had tried to be that son. She rode well, hunted, fished, and shot like an expert. She preferred the company of men, for she knew she alarmed women, whereas men accepted her, she thought, as an equal.

The other light in Mira's life was Lord Charles Devere, younger son of the Duke of Barshire. He was ten years older than she, but it had amused him to take the child, Mira, fishing and hunting. He had gone away to join the army but had written to her from time to time from the Peninsular wars, and Mira had followed every battle in the newspapers and pestered every military gentleman who visited her parents for details.

Lord Charles had been absent at the wars for four years, and Mira missed him dreadfully.

One winter's day as she returned from a hard day's hunting, she was thinking of him and of what fun they once had together. Muddy and windswept, she erupted into the elegance of the Markhams' drawing room, where Drusilla sat at the harp, admiring the effect of the rise and fall of her own white arms.

'How many times must I tell you,' said Mrs. Markham wearily, 'to change before you enter my drawing room? Go and put on a clean gown and return here immediately. Your father wishes to speak to you.'

Mira's green eyes flew anxiously to her father, but he was reading a newspaper and did not look up.

She went upstairs and allowed the maid she shared with Drusilla to help her into a gown after she had washed and to try to tease some semblance of order into her frizzy, windswept hair.

Mira descended to the drawing room by sliding down the banisters. As usual, the minute she entered, despite the fact that she was wearing a fashionable gown, she felt gauche and dowdy. Drusilla was always calm and impeccable. Mrs. Markham, who had once been as beautiful as Drusilla, moved gracefully, talked in a low, pleasant voice, and tried hard not to disturb her appearance with any evidence of animation whatsoever. Mr. Markham was slim and elegantly tailored as if for a London salon rather than a country drawing room.

'Sit down, Mira,' said Mr. Markham. Mira sat down wide-eyed, unused to any attention from her father.

'As you know, Mira,' said Mr. Markham, delicately taking a pinch of snuff, 'we are to take Drusilla to London for her come-out. She is nineteen and you are eighteen. We originally planned that should she be engaged after the next Season—and we are confident that she will be—you should make your own come-out the following Season.'

3

'To which I have strongly objected. Money on a Season for Mira would be sadly wasted,' said Mrs. Markham.

'But,' went on Mr. Markham, as if his wife had not spoken, 'I have decided to bring you out together.'

'I agree with Mama,' said Mira roundly. 'I would not take.'

'I must protest, Mr. Markham.' His wife looked fondly at the beautiful Drusilla. 'Mira is a hoyden. Besides, what gentleman is even going to look at her beside Drusilla?'

Does Mama even realize how very cruel she is being? thought Mira. Aloud she said, 'It is very kind of you, Papa, but in truth I do not need a Season, and I should dislike it above all things.'

'Nonetheless, you will go.' Her father's voice was flat and final.

Mrs. Markham began to protest again, but he picked up a newspaper and paid no heed to her complaints. Drusilla smiled at Mira maliciously. 'It might be fun,' she said. 'We shall have such larks.' Drusilla, after her initial surprise that her father should be so determined that Mira have a Season, was beginning to relish the idea. Her own beauty and grace set against Mira's undistinguished looks and clumsy manners could only be enhanced by the contrast.

But Mira had had one thing in her young life that Drusilla had coveted, and that was her friendship with Lord Charles Devere. Although she knew that it had obviously amused the older Lord Charles to make a playmate of the boyish Mira, it had rankled that he seemed to find her, Drusilla, somewhat tiresome.

But she knew she had grown in beauty and was no longer the rather chubby little girl he had known. She had also just heard from her parents that he was returning on leave and would be at the Season. A rather calculating look entered her eyes as she looked at Mira. It would serve Mira right if her precious Lord Charles barely noticed her. Drusilla did not know that she was jealous of her sister, jealous of Mira's popularity with the men on the hunting field and with the people of Darton, the nearby market town.

She had not meant to tell Mira about Lord Charles's forthcoming visit to London in case it encouraged the girl to prettify herself in any way or to modify her hurly-burly manners, but Mrs. Markham said suddenly, 'Lord Charles is coming home on leave.'

Mira's green eyes suddenly shone like emeralds. 'He is coming home? How soon? Oh, how wonderful it will be to see him again.'

'He is going directly to London,' said Mrs. Markham. 'He will be at the Season.'

Mira's face fell and then lit up. 'But we can still have fun. He is like me. The fashionable life bores him. We can go and see the

5

waxworks. We can—'

Mrs. Markham's voice cut through her enthusiasm. 'Lord Charles is coming to the Season to find a wife.'

Mira looked at her, startled. In her innocence she had never thought of Charles marrying. Then she rallied. Everything would be all right once she saw him again.

*　　　*　　　*

But somehow in the weeks that followed, Mira thought she would never see him again. The weather was bad. It rained incessantly, steady, drenching rain, thudding on the roof of her family mansion and chuckling in the lead gutters. The nearby River Blyn overflowed its banks, and Mira got a sound dressing down from her mother for going out to help the flooded townspeople while she was wearing the masculine clothes she wore on the hunting field. In fact, so alarmed was Mrs. Markham at Mira's dress and behavior that a lady of quality fallen on hard times called Mrs. Dunstable was hired to school Mira in grace, deportment, and conversation. So Mira found her freedom ruthlessly cut off, and it was only at night when she slid down the apple tree outside her window dressed in breeches and coat and made her way across the rain-soggy lawns that she felt she could breathe.

A month before their departure to London

was due, she made her escape as usual during the night. When she was out of sight of the large, square mansion with the porticoed entrance that was her home, she took off her hat and let the rain fall on her straightened hair. She hated the hair straightener—which her mother had insisted the maid apply—with a passion, for it made her scalp itch dreadfully.

It was made in the stillroom from one pound of beef suet, two ounces of yellow wax, two ounces of castor oil, twelve grains of benzoic acid, thirty drops of oil of lemon, and five drops of oil of cinnamon. The preparation was massaged through her hair twice a day so that it would lie flat.

She made her way across the soggy lawns. The rain of the previous weeks had eased off to a thin drizzle. She jumped over a stile and entered the darkness of the home wood. Here was where she had often walked and talked with Charles. Surely he would return home after this dreadful Season, and then they would walk and talk again.

She bit her lip. But he might be married! Charles, married! And then her heart began to beat hard. Perhaps he could marry her, and then everything would be as it was. She could go to the army with him when he rejoined his regiment, and they would have such adventures. And she would refuse to let the maid straighten her hair again. She should appear as he remembered her. Besides, her

7

frizzy hair was at least healthy and shiny, whereas the straightening made it look dark and dull.

So Mira walked on under the dripping trees of the home wood, surrounded by the comforting wet smell of old leaves, wrapped in a fantasy about marriage to Charles—which was, in her unawakened mind, more like a schoolboy adventure than a romance.

*   *   *

The next day Mira's rebellion over her hair was unexpectedly supported by her father. Mr. Markham cut through his wife's protests by saying firmly, 'Her hair is better frizzy. It looks unhealthy with that stuff on it. Leave it.' And as Mr. Markham's word was law, that was that. Looking at him, Mira thought there was a gleam of amusement and affection in his normally cold gray eyes, but she immediately decided she must have been mistaken.

But Drusilla had noticed it, too, and was jealous. She had further reason to be jealous. The townspeople and neighbors were sending presents to Mira, wishing her well in London, and Lady Rother, who lived on the far side of the town, had sent a present of a handsome fan on ivory sticks, which Drusilla coveted. She simply could not understand Lady Rother's behavior, for ladies were apt to shy away from Mira, and Lady Rother was a high stickler. She

8

did not know, and neither did Mira, that Lady Rother had been touched by the report of Mira's help during the flooding and had decided the girl had 'bottom', which was better than looks any day.

So during the days before they were due to depart to London, Drusilla tried her best to undermine Mira's confidence by sighing sympathetically over her sister's lack of style and looks. But Mira hardly paid any attention to her. The prospect of London had a whole new magic for her now that she knew she was to see her beloved Charles again.

Slowly the house began to empty. The Markhams had rented a town house in St. James's Square. Most of the servants and a fourgon piled high with luggage were sent on first, and then the great day arrived. It was sunny at last, with a warm spring wind drying the grass and buds appearing on the bare branches of the trees, when the Markham family finally set out.

They were to arrive some weeks before the beginning of the Season so that Mrs. Markham could 'nurse the ground'—that is, meet the most important of the London hostesses and so secure invitations to balls and parties for her daughters.

Mrs. Markham often wondered why her husband was incurring such unnecessary expense in giving Mira a Season. Still, she reflected, as Mira would possibly remain unwed, it was only right that the girl should have some fun. Her unruly ways would quieten with age, and she might become a pleasant, if spinster, companion to her parents in their declining years. But, ah, Drusilla! Mrs. Markham looked fondly at her elder daughter's rather petulant face under the fashionable bonnet. Drusilla would break hearts.

They stayed two nights at posting houses on the road, finally entering the outskirts of London in the morning. Drusilla shrank back against the squabs. London was so large, so noisy, and so very grimy, it was not what she had expected at all. But Mira sat forward in her seat, her green eyes shining. Charles was in London, and so everything about London was beautiful—from the billboards advertising Warren's blacking to the multitude of shops at the East End of the city, which had not yet been glassed in like the more fashionable ones of the West End but had their many-colored wares spilling out into the streets.

But Drusilla began to brighten as the quieter streets and squares of the West End were reached. She peered from the window of the carriage, studying the dress of the ladies and commenting on the height of cravats worn by the dandies.

Mira expected that Charles would call almost as soon as they were settled in, but when he did not, she contented herself by believing he would call the following day.

But a week of calls on various ladies went by, a stultifying week to Mira of boring conversation at boring tea tables, and still he did not call. Another week passed and then another, and Mira began to feel desperate. The rigid modes and manners of London society were becoming terrifying to her, and the more she thought of attending her first ball, the more clumsy and gauche she became. She even began to regret that her mentor, Mrs. Dunstable, had not come to London with them.

And then two days before their first ball, Mira heard her father remark that he had met Lord Charles at the club the preceding afternoon.

'But why hasn't he called?' she cried.

Her father rustled his paper impatiently. 'Lord Charles has many friends and acquaintances in London. He has been too busy. You will see him at your first ball. He is to attend.'

'Where is he residing?' asked Drusilla.

'He has lodgings in South Audley Street next to the Welsh bakery,' said Mr. Markham.

All that long day Mira worried and worried. If only she could see Charles, if only she could reassure herself that he still cared for her. And then she remembered her masculine clothes, which she had brought from the country and hidden in the back of the press in her room.

Her heart beat with excitement. She could slip out the following morning before anyone was awake and go and see him. How he would laugh!

She barely slept that night. Surely Charles would not be so silly as to keep fashionable hours and not rise until two in the afternoon. At nine in the morning she slipped out of the house in her breeches and coat with a hat jammed down over her hair. She began to swagger, enjoying the old freedom of pretending to be a boy.

But when she reached the corner of South Audley Street, her steps began to falter. Everything was so quiet, not a fashionable to be seen. But surely it would be all right when she saw Charles again. She found the bakery, went to the house next door to it, and faced a row of doorbells that looked like organ stops. Which one was Charles's? She retreated to the bakery, which was fortunately open, and said boldly, 'Delivery for Lord Charles Devere. Which is his apartment?'

'Number three,' said the baker laconically, and went back to picking his teeth.

Mira went back, drew a deep breath, and pulled the bell marked with a brass three. Somewhere deep in the silent building, a bell jangled noisily on its wire. She waited and waited and then heard the sound of advancing footsteps.

The door was opened by a servant in black

12

coat, knee breeches, and striped waistcoat.

'What is it, lad?' he demanded.

'I am called to see Lord Charles,' said Mira haughtily.

'Be off with you.'

'Tell Lord Charles that Miss Mira Markham is called to see him.'

The servant's eyes widened slightly, and then his gaze raked up and down her clothes. His eyes returned slowly to her face. Mira stared him down.

'Follow me, miss,' he said curtly.

He led the way to the first floor, opened a door that led into a hallway, and said, 'Be so good as to wait there.'

Mira took off her hat and twisted the brim round in her fingers. The flat was dark and silent, with only faint noises of traffic from the street below filtering up through the gloom.

She heard the low murmur of voices from a room, and then the servant reappeared. Again he said, 'Follow me' and this time led her into a masculine-looking study. 'His lordship will be with you presently,' he said.

Mira sat down nervously and looked about her. There was a business-like desk against the window and several shiny black leather and horsehair-filled chairs like the one on which she was perched. There was a large oil painting on the wall depicting a hunting scene and several smaller oils of horses. A stand in the corner held an assortment of whips, sticks, and riding crops. Stuck into the gold frame of the mirror over the fireplace were many invitations.

There was a console table at her elbow with copies of *The Sporting Life* and *The Gentleman's Magazine*. She flicked open *The Gentleman's Magazine* and tried to find something to read.

There was an article called 'Observations on Hunting by the Late King of Prussia,' which seemed very boring even to an enthusiastic hunter like herself. She settled down to read a chilling article titled 'Calculations on the Game of Life and Death.'

The article claimed that half of all people born in the British Isles died before they reached the age of seventeen. More girls than boys died of the smallpox, it went on, and just as Mira had reached the bit where it explained cheerfully that most deaths could be expected to take place in March, the door opened and Lord Charles strode in. He was unshaven and wrapped in an oriental dressing gown, and his black hair was ruffled.

Mira threw down the magazine and jumped to her feet with a glad cry of welcome, a cry that died on her lips when she saw the look of horror on his face.

'What on earth are you doing here?' demanded Charles. 'And dressed like a guy?'

'But . . . but I wanted to see you,' said Mira. 'And you were used to seeing me in boys'

14

clothes.'

His blue eyes stared down at her. 'That was when you were a child. Unless I am much mistaken, you are in London for your come-out.'

'Yes, but . . . but . . .'

'Then this is no way to go on.'

'But we are friends,' wailed Mira, 'and London is so strange and, in fact, quite terrifying. I thought perhaps we might have some fun. I have not been to the Tower.'

'I think you should concentrate on getting your manners ready for your come-out,' said Charles, 'instead of hankering after unfashionable places.'

She looked uneasily at his handsome, regular features. 'You are changed, Charles.'

His manner softened. 'You are a shameless scapegrace, Mira. Off with you before your parents find out what you have been up to.' He ruffled her frizzy hair. 'I shall see you at your very first ball. It is at the Henrys', is it not?'

Mira dumbly nodded. Charles picked up a small brass bell and rang it, and when his servant answered its summons, he said, 'Show Miss Mira out, James, and forget you ever saw her here.'

Mira got up and followed the servant to the door. On the threshold she turned around, 'Charles . . .' she began. But he said impatiently, 'Go, and go quickly before you are seen.'

15

Outside she stood on the pavement, irresolute. A newspaper blew along the street and wrapped itself around her legs. She tore it away and then with her hands in her pockets slowly began to make her way home.

When she reached home, she was lucky in that there were no servants in the hall, so she was able to scamper up the stairs to her room, unobserved. She threw herself face-down on the bed, but she did not cry. Her mind searched desperately for an explanation for her beloved Charles's cold behavior. And then she realized with shame that this was, after all, London, and it had been very shocking indeed to call on him at his home and dressed in such a way. Her childhood was behind her, never to return.

*　　　*　　　*

The eve of the ball rushed on her in a last-minute flurry of dancing instructions and dress rehearsals. She could not help but become excited. Mira had never paid much attention to dress before, but now she was glad that her ball gown was so pretty. It was of white muslin, the finest India muslin, worn over a white silk underdress. There were so many intricate flounces at the hem that it seemed to foam about her feet when she walked.

Finally they were ready to set out, and Mira was so caught up at the idea of Charles seeing her in her finery that she did not notice that Drusilla was looking exceptionally beautiful. Although the Markhams lived in a fairly grand style in the country, Mira was startled at the magnificence of Lord and Lady Henry's mansion in Grosvenor Square, where the ball was being held. Lights blazed from top to bottom of the house. As they entered the wide hallway with its black-and-white tiles, she saw that the very hall was decorated with hangings of silk and banks of hothouse flowers. A double line of footmen in livery lined the wide staircase that led up to the chain of saloons on the first floor, which had been turned into a ballroom for the evening.

They left their cloaks and joined Mr. Markham at the foot of the stairs. As they began to mount, Mira tried not to be afraid. Charles would be there. He would smile at her and dance with her, and after that everything would be all right.

She and Drusilla curtsied to Lord and Lady Henry and then followed their mother and father into the ballroom. Their entrance excited a certain commotion, and Mira realized that quizzing glasses were being trained on her sister's beauty. But what did it matter what the gentlemen thought of her sister? Charles had always rated her a tiresome little girl.

After Mr. and Mrs. Markham had circled the floor, chatting to friends and

17

acquaintances, Mr. Markham went off to the card room, and Mrs. Markham and her daughters sat down on gilt rout chairs at the edge of the floor, where dancers were performing the quadrille.

Just as that dance ended, Mira saw Charles entering the ballroom, and her heart turned over. He looked so handsome in formal black. Surely there was no man in London who looked better.

And he saw her, sitting there with her mother and Drusilla, and he smiled and began to make his way toward them.

Mira's green eyes shone as she watched him approach. All her social unease, all her uncertainties melted away. She knew herself to be a good dancer, better than Drusilla.

And then just as Charles was nearly at their side, his eyes fell on Drusilla, who smiled at him, a little curved smile. She lowered her long lashes and slowly waved her fan.

Charles bowed, and the ladies rose and curtsied. Charles had forgotten Mira's very existence. His blue eyes were fastened on Drusilla's face. 'Can this be little Drusilla?' he asked.

'My daughter has grown in looks,' said Mrs. Markham.

Charles appeared to collect his wits. He bowed again in front of Drusilla. 'Miss Markham,' he said, 'would you do me the very great honor of partnering me in this next dance?'

With one single graceful movement, Drusilla, lifted her train over her arm, and put her gloved fingers on the arm Charles was holding out.

'Delighted,' she murmured.

They moved off together, and Mira sat down again suddenly, her mind one black pit of misery. What did fun and companionship matter when one did not possess beauty?

A young man came up to Mira and asked her to dance. She accepted, but all the time her eyes followed Charles and Drusilla, so that by the end of the dance, she could neither remember the name of the man she had danced with nor remember what he looked like. Misery made her look grim-faced, and so she was to have very few partners that evening. Charles showed no sign of wanting to dance with her. He danced twice with Drusilla and then spent quite a lot of time leaning against a pillar and watching her.

When they all went in for refreshments, Mira walked beside her mother, a great anger against her sister rising in her tortured bosom.

In the center of the room that was being used for refreshments, there was a fountain surrounded by a wide, shallow pool in which goldfish darted. Drusilla was standing there with a young man, laughing and flirting.

A friend of Mrs. Markham's called to her, and so with her mother's attention elsewhere,

19

Mira marched straight up to her sister and said belligerently, 'I want a word with you.'

The young man bowed and retreated. 'What is it, sis?' asked Drusilla languidly.

'I want you to leave Charles alone,' said Mira. 'You can have any gentleman you like. Leave Charles for me.'

'You silly widgeon,' said Drusilla. 'Lord Charles is not in the slightest interested in you. He has asked Mama's permission to take me out driving, and I am going. So there!'

Never had Mira known such sick jealousy. The room seemed to swim about her and her hands to move of their own volition as she suddenly pushed her sister backward, so that Drusilla, with a loud shriek, fell into the pool.

Mira stood stricken, wondering whether she had run mad. Voices all about her were crying, 'Shame!' Gentlemen were helping a now weeping Drusilla from the pool. Her soaking dress was clinging to her body, serving to make Drusilla appear even more entrancing in the eyes of the gentlemen.

And then Mira heard Charles's voice at her ear, saying with bitter contempt, 'You are a disgusting hoyden, Mira. I am ashamed of you!'

Then Mr. Markham was there to say the carriage had been summoned. Drusilla must be taken home immediately before she caught a chill. Voices rose and fell about Mira's now scarlet little ears, voices exclaiming in condemnation at her behavior.

Mr. Markham said nothing until they were home and Drusilla, wrapped in blankets, had been carried up to bed to be fussed over by her mother and the servants.

'In here,' he said curtly to Mira, holding open the door of the library. Head bowed, Mira slowly walked in.

'Will you send me home?' she asked.

'That is what you deserve,' he said coldly. 'Mrs. Markham is most insisted on it. She suggests you be returned to Mrs. Dunstable and confined to the house. I do not like failures, Mira, and you are not only a social disgrace but a social failure. Because Lord Charles Devere spoiled you by paying attention to you when you were a child does not mean he is going to trouble his head now with a hurly-burly miss. You will have, however, a chance to redeem yourself. You are to be kept indoors here for two weeks, two weeks in which you will study dancing, deportment, and manners. You have been over-indulged as a child and allowed to run wild.'

Mira wanted to cry out, 'But I did it for you. You wanted a son. I tried to be that son.' But one did not express one's feelings to one's parents, and so she stood there, feeling her world about her lying in ruins. She felt too weak to protest, too weak to say that after what she had done, she could not face one member

21

of London society.

'You may go,' said Mr. Markham, and Mira turned and ran from the room, ran to the sanctuary of her bedroom, feeling a tight pain in her chest made by the tears that would not come, for the disgrace and the hurt were too much for tears.

CHAPTER TWO

To Mira the following week was a species of hell. She stood at the window and watched Drusilla driving off with Charles, saw the glow of admiration in his eyes as he looked at her sister, saw bleakly the way Drusilla flirted with him. Then in the evenings there was all the fuss as preparations were made to take Drusilla to some ball or party. When she drove off with her parents, Mira was left alone with the servants to reflect on her social disgrace.

Because of her one burst of temper, Charles was out there, at all the balls and parties attended by Drusilla and every other pretty girl in society, and she could only torture herself with thoughts of what he would say, how he would look, and how little he probably thought of her.

Mira was even banned from the drawing room when Drusilla's admirers came to call, and then at the end of that first week, she heard Mrs. Markham say complacently, 'Lord Charles is only the younger son of a duke, but he will do very well for Drusilla. Has he asked you yet for permission to pay his addresses?' And Mr. Markham replied in an amused voice, 'Not yet. But he will. He will.'

Mira began to move about in a dream of what it had been like in the past, remembering Charles's every word and expression.

At the beginning of the second week, the weather was still unexpectedly fine, and Drusilla and her parents set off to a picnic in the Surrey fields. Mira was told to practise her scales on the pianoforte. She itched for freedom, and though she had sworn never to don masculine clothes again, she put them on, hung over the banisters, and waited until the hall was empty of servants, and then slipped out into the London streets.

Somehow she found her steps taking her in the direction of South Audley Street. Although she knew Charles would probably be at the picnic, she had a sick desire to stand outside his house and to walk on the same pavement he walked on every day. But there was something cheering about the weather, about the sunshine and the scudding little breeze, which drove white clouds across a blue sky far above the grimy chimney pots of London.

She turned into Grosvenor Square and was halfway round it when she stopped to listen to a noisy altercation. A tall gentleman with

23

arresting good looks and a powerful figure was berating a protesting groom. The groom was saying that he did not know where my lord's tiger had got to, and my lord was complaining crossly that he was due at a curricle race and needed his tiger.

Afterward Mira blamed the sunshine and the light breeze, which appeared to have made her reckless. There was also the desire not to be shamed Mira, the social disgrace, but someone else entirely.

She marched boldly up to the curricle, pulling her hat firmly down over her eyes as she did so, and said in what she hoped was a Cockney accent, 'I'll be yer tiger, my lord.'

A pair of cold gray eyes stared down at her. 'Experience, lad?'

'Tiger to Mr. Markham, sir, of St. James's Square.'

'Very well. Hop up. I have wasted enough time as it is. But if you prove not to know what you are doing, you will get a whipping.'

Mira sprang nimbly onto the backstrap and hung on for dear life as the carriage surged forward. They went as far as a point on the Great West Road just beyond the village of Knightsbridge, where her driver slowed his team and joined several other drivers and carriages. She dutifully nipped down and ran to the horses' heads. She discovered from overhearing the conversation that her driver was the Marquess of Grantley. The diminutive tiger holding the heads of a team of horses next to her jeered, 'Can't your master buy you a livery?'

''Is tiger's sick,' drawled Mira laconically. 'Standing in.'

Then she found her temporary master looking down at her. 'Name?' he demanded.

'Jem,' said Mira.

'Well, Jem, we are about ready to start.'

Mira was never to forget that race. Never had she been driven so fast. Houses and nursery gardens and then countryside seemed to pass in a blur. They were ahead of the others almost from the start, and Mira shouted and yelled with exhilaration, all her worries forgotten.

When they drove into an inn yard after the marquess had easily won the race, Mira felt she was Jem and that sad girl Mira was someone she had once known. She jumped down and ran to the horses' heads, and then when the marquess had climbed down, she expertly unhitched the team of four and said, 'I will see they are rubbed down, my lord, and watered.'

'Good lad,' he said. 'The job is yours if you want it,' and without waiting for a reply, he strode into the inn.

Mira saw to the horses, glad now that so much of her misspent youth had been passed in the stables.

Then one of the other tigers approached

her. He was a wizened little fellow with a twisted white face. He looked as if he had been born old.

'Your master cheated,' he said.

Color rose in Mira's face. 'We won fair and square!'

'Cheated! Cheated!' jeered the tiger. The other tigers and grooms gathered around.

'You lying churl,' said Mira haughtily, forgetting her role and her Cockney accent.

'Put up yer fists,' growled the tiger.

'A mill! A mill!' shouted the onlookers gleefully, and began to lay bets.

The marquess, emerging from the inn, saw with some amusement that his new tiger was squaring up in the inn yard for a fight. The tigers were crying to Mira to take off her coat, and she was refusing, clutching it tightly about her. One boy tried to tear the coat off her back, but she jerked herself away and shrugged it back on—but not before the startled marquess had caught a fleeting glimpse of a very female bosom.

He marched forward, seized Mira by the scruff of her neck, and frog-marched her off to his carriage, shouting over his shoulder to the onlookers, 'I have no time for brawls.' He tossed a guinea to a watching groom. 'Fetch my team and hitch them up.'

The groom stared in awe at the gold and then ran off to get his horses. The marquess kept his hold on Mira. 'You stay exactly where you are,' he said softly. When his team was hitched, he ordered curtly, 'Jump up,' and the terrified Mira, who felt she really ought to run away, obeyed him.

He drove off for a little way and then cut off the gravel surface of the Great West Road and down a leafy country lane. He finally commanded his team to stop. Mira jumped down and ran to their heads, hoping against hope that if she continued in her role, her true identity would remain undiscovered.

That hope died when he snatched off her cap. Her frizzy hair sprang out about her face like an aureole. Wide green eyes stared helplessly up into gray ones.

'So, Miss What's-your-name, explain yourself.'

Mira hung her head. 'I was amusing myself,' she said.

'Who are you?'

'I am Mira Markham, and I am in London for my first Season.'

'And is this the way you go about trying to find suitors?'

'No, my lord.'

'So you do know who I am?'

'I overheard your name. But I did not know who you were in Grosvenor Square.' Mira put her head back and looked up at him bravely. 'I was not tricking you in order to attract you, my lord. My heart belongs to another.'

'Indeed?' The voice was warmer now,

amused. 'I trust you will be very happy.'

To Mira's horror a large, fat tear rolled from one of her eyes and slid down her cheek.

'Get back in the carriage,' said the marquess. 'I would like to hear your story.'

He drove sedately back to the main road and then stopped at an inn outside Knightsbridge. He told Mira to put on her cap and then ushered her inside. He ordered wine for himself and lemonade for Mira.

'Now, Miss Mira,' he began, 'what is all this about?'

He was very handsome, with golden hair curling under a curly brimmed beaver. He was tall and powerful, with a trim waist and long legs encased in leather breeches and top boots. But Mira could think only of Charles, and for the first time in his privileged life, the Marquess of Grantley was facing a young female who was not interested in him in the slightest.

Mira glanced up at him fleetingly. She had beautiful eyes, he thought, like jewels. In a halting voice she began to tell him about Charles, her voice warming as she talked about the old days, when she had still been a child and they had gone hunting and fishing together. Never had anyone, not even Charles, listened so intently to Mira before. She told him of her desire to please her father by trying to be a son to him. And then she told him about Drusilla and the disastrous ball and then about her social disgrace. His eyes sparkled with laughter. 'You are a terror, Miss Mira. So when do you come out of seclusion?'

'There is another ball to be held at Lord Monday's. I am to go there.'

'But not Almack's Assembly Rooms?'

Mira shook her head. 'Mama had applied for vouchers, but the patronesses are so very strict, and because of my disgrace the vouchers were refused. Drusilla is furious with me. Oh, all this marriage-market business is so silly.'

'And yet you would not find it silly if it secured Lord Charles for you.'

Her face looked wistful. 'I am not beautiful. I have no hope now.'

The marquess found himself bitterly damning Lord Charles and the Markham family. This girl had character, a piquant face, and a beautiful mouth. 'You yourself,' he realized Mira was saying, 'have escaped marriage.'

'Not at all,' he replied. 'I was married young, but my wife died after we had been married only two years. She died in childbirth.'

'How sad! I am so very sorry.'

'That was some time ago.'

'Are you going to tell my parents what I have done?' asked Mira.

'No, it is up to you to return unobserved.'

'I do not know how to thank you. You are most . . . tolerant.'

'You amuse me, Miss Mira. I shall be at the

Mondays' ball. I will dance with you if you promise not to push me into any fountains.'

'I will never do such a thing again!'

'Good. And I shall be interested to see the *dramatis personae* in this comedy.'

'Comedy to you, my lord. Tragedy to me.'

'Everything is a tragedy at your age, my chuck.'

'But everyone will be looking at me and whispering.'

'Society loves characters, although, I admit, it has to be the men who are the characters. But if you remain pleasant and do not extinguish that liveliness of spirit you obviously possess, you will attain a certain notoriety, and that is no bad thing.'

'Charles will not even look at me.'

'If you consider yourself deeply sunk in disgrace, then Lord Charles and society will take you at your own valuation. It seems to me you have a great deal of physical courage. Now is the time for you to find reserves of moral courage. You are far from plain. You have a neat figure, splendid eyes, and good skin. Remember that.'

Mira looked at him in humble gratitude. 'I had become used to thinking myself plain.'

'If you think yourself plain, then that is how you will look. Now I must get you home, for I fear if this adventure is discovered, then you will be in the suds and confined to your room for the rest of the Season.'

They drove back to London in amiable silence. When they reached the corner of St. James's Square, where he had planned to drop her, Mira let out an exclamation of dismay. Her parents' carriage had just arrived.

'My family is returned,' she wailed. 'What am I to do?'

'Is there a back way into the house?'

'Yes, there is a door from the garden at the back.'

'Off with you. I will find someone to guard my horses and then create a diversion.'

Mira scampered off across the square. The marquess found one of the grooms from the nearby mews to hold his horses. He went up to the Markhams' house, rapped on the door, and said to the surprised butler who answered it, 'Fire on your roof! Get everyone out.'

The butler promptly turned and began shouting, 'Fire!' at the top of his voice. 'Everyone outside,' urged the marquess as scared servants followed by Mr. and Mrs. Markham and some beauty he judged to be Drusilla came crowding into the hall.

Meanwhile Mira had scrambled over the wall at the back. She heard the commotion coming faintly and cries of 'Fire!' She quietly slipped in by the garden door, ran up the stairs to her room, tore off her masculine clothes, and with shaking hands put on a gown. She tidied her hair with trembling fingers and then ran back down the stairs and out the front door with the last of the servants to where everyone else was gathered in the square. She stared up at the roof in time to hear the marquess say, 'I am most sorry to have alarmed you. It must have been a brief chimney fire. Still, it is better to be safe than sorry.'

'Indeed, yes,' agreed Mr. Markham, who had just learned the identity of his would-be deliverer from danger. Marquesses must always be believed; it was only the common people whose word one doubted.

'We are most grateful to you, my lord,' said Drusilla, dimpling up at him.

He smiled at her and said, 'Alas, no beauty in distress to rescue. No knight errant, I. Good day to you all. You are fortunate, Mr. Markham, in having two such beautiful daughters.' He bowed before Mira and whispered, 'Your boots are showing under your gown,' straightened up, and with a casual wave of his hand strolled off.

Mira turned and hurried indoors so that she could get rid of her boots before her parents noticed. It was only much later that day that she reflected on the happenings of it and realized with a little surge of gratitude that she had found a new friend.

All that the marquess had said to her about moral courage turned over and over in her brain, and Mrs. Markham said with some surprise to her husband that little Mira was taking an interest in clothes at last.

And it was Mira who said she did not want to wear feathers in her hair to the Mondays' ball, those tall osprey feathers dyed different colors. She said she was too short and that she had read that a garland of fresh flowers was considered very fashionable and she would prefer that. Drusilla gave her a little, curved, complacent smile. She knew she herself had the height to carry a headdress of feathers, and besides, when had little Mira had any idea of how to go on?

Mr. Markham ordered that Mira was to have her way. But Mira, who had been feeling confident, for she knew she would see the marquess there, began to feel uneasy again. For when she made calls with her mother and Drusilla on the various London hostesses, the talk was suddenly all about the Marquess of Grantley, how handsome he was, how rich, how he had never 'done' the Season since the death of his wife, and how he was rated the best catch on the marriage market. Mira was all too aware of Drusilla's increased interest in this marquess and saw how eagerly she regaled the ladies with a story about how the kind marquess had warned them of a fire and how warmly he had looked at her. And the ladies smiled indulgently, for Drusilla was already being talked of as the belle of the Season. Despite her beauty the hostesses, with daughters of their own to puff off, treated her with indulgence, for she prattled on in a light

33

manner about all sorts of trivial things, and that was their idea of the perfect young lady. Mira they regarded with suspicion. There was, they said to one another, something of the caged animal about the girl. Farouche, yes definitely farouche.

But Mira clung grimly onto the idea of moral courage and for once told the lady's maid that she shared with Drusilla to allow plenty of time to prepare her for the ball. Then came the first battle. The lady's maid, Betty, complained that it would be too difficult to arrange fresh flowers in Mira's hair and that she should wear a turban, a Juliet cap, or feathers. To Mrs. Markham's amazement Mira promptly demanded the services of a top hairdresser, saying that if she was to salvage her reputation, then she ought to appear at her best.

Drusilla waited for Mr. Markham to tell this unruly daughter to behave herself, but to her mortification Mr. Markham said in an amused voice, 'Then order one, Mira, and let us all have some peace.'

Mira grandly summoned Monsieur Duval, the court hairdresser, unaware that if that temperamental artist had not had his services canceled by the Duchess of Rowcester at the last minute, then he would not have been able to attend.

And so Mira had a wreath of ivy and camellias, the latest hothouse flower, decorating her head. Her gown of white muslin had a green sprig, and her evening gloves were a soft green kid. The high waist of the gown was bound by a broad green silk sash. There was something almost fairylike about Mira, thought Mr. Markham in surprise. Drusilla glared at her sister, trying to tell herself that Mira looked like a guy but not quite succeeding. Her own headdress of tall feathers gave her a stately air, or so she told herself, although she was already beginning to find it cumbersome. The feathers were admittedly light, but it was the heavy gold fillet to which they were attached that made her head ache a little.

Another grand house, another grand staircase, another ballroom full of staring eyes. This must be what hell is like, thought Mira, eyes and eyes and more eyes, all calculating and disapproving.

She was standing with her mother and Drusilla at the edge of the floor when the marquess came up to them. He smiled at Mira and said, 'The honor of this dance?'

Before Mira could speak, Drusilla said, 'Most certainly, my lord,' and put her hand on his arm.

'Miss Markham,' he said gently. 'A mistake. My invitation was meant for your sister.'

Drusilla blushed painfully and retreated to her mother's side. Beside them, listening avidly to every word, was a Mrs. Gardener, one of

London's greatest gossips. Mira tripped off lightly with the marquess, and soon they were dancing a waltz, Mira demonstrating to society and to her jaundiced sister that she was an exquisite dancer. But at one moment her steps faltered, and the marquess pressed her hand tightly. 'No, don't tell me,' he said. 'I can guess: Lord Charles is arrived, so now you must dance your best, not trip over my feet. And, no, you must not look at him even once!'

Lord Charles went straight up to Drusilla and bowed before her. 'Will I be lucky to secure the next dance?'

'What? Oh, yes, I suppose so,' said Drusilla, her eyes fastened on the dancing Mira.

Lord Charles turned away from her and put up his quizzing glass to see what was claiming her attention. He saw Mira dancing with an exceptionally handsome man, whom she seemed to be keeping well amused.

'Who is Mira's partner?' he asked.

'The Marquess of Grantley,' said Drusilla sulkily.

'Indeed! He is said to be the catch of the Season.'

'I don't see why. He is quite old,' said Drusilla sulkily. And Lord Charles, who judged the marquess to be not much older than he was himself, looked at her in surprise.

'It is a good thing he has chosen to dance with her before anyone else,' said Charles, unwittingly putting another log on Drusilla's already smoldering anger, 'because he will give her some much-needed social cachet.'

The waltz finished, Mira was promenading round the ballroom with the marquess. 'You dance very prettily,' he said.

'Thank you, my lord,' replied Mira in an abstracted way. 'You dance very prettily yourself.'

'Now you are not to sit out and cast languishing looks at Lord Charles,' he said severely. 'Try for a bit of dignity.'

Mira gave a little sigh. 'If only he would look at me the way he looks at Drusilla.'

He experienced a stab of irritation. He had always been courted and fêted. He was not used to spending time with any young female who was plainly sighing for someone else. On the other hand he was sorry for her. He would secure her for the supper dance, take her in to supper, demonstrate to the fashionable world that he found Miss Mira Markham charming, and then forget about her.

And Mira would have remained relatively happy that evening had not Charles, after his dance with Drusilla, asked her to dance. It was the quadrille, something she usually danced very well, but his very presence distracted her so that she stumbled several times. It was like a poison seeping back into her blood, her longing for his attention. She hated the way the elegant figures of the dance separated them and made conversation impossible. When she

37

promenaded with him at the end of the dance, she searched to re-establish the old camaraderie with him, but she noticed his eyes kept straying to where Drusilla was walking with *her* partner.

He delivered her back to Mrs. Markham, and Mira sat down primly, back very straight, trying to look cheerful but feeling only loss and misery welling up in her.

But where the great Marquess of Grantley led, others followed, and to Mira's surprise a gentleman immediately approached and asked her for the next dance and so it went on until the fact that she was demonstrating not only to Charles but to her father how popular she had become raised her spirits. She was intelligent enough to know the reason for her sudden popularity, and when the marquess secured her hand for another waltz, this time the supper one, she smiled up at him with open friendliness and said, 'Thank you for restoring me to the good graces of society.'

'You are welcome. Are you enjoying the ball?'

'I would enjoy it better if Charles would stop pining after Drusilla.'

'I will talk to you about this at supper.'

Mrs. Markham looked at Mira in startled surprise as the marquess led her younger daughter into the supper room. Other mothers of hopefuls were congratulating her rather sourly on Mira's 'success'.

'Now,' began the marquess severely, when Mira had been served with food and wine, 'pay attention to me, and stop letting your eyes wander past my shoulder in case your beloved Charles should hove into view. It strikes me that the amiable Charles amused himself by being kind to a child. For some immature reason you expected that friendship to go on. But now you are a young woman and must put away childish dreams. You are not going to get your childhood companion back, no matter what happens. You should begin your bereavement now and stop wasting time hoping that he will pay attention to you. You probably do not even think of him as a woman thinks of a man. You do not dream of kisses but of days on the hunting field. So it should be easy for you to forget him. You are not in love.'

'I am *deeply* in love,' protested Mira. 'You cannot see inside my head.'

'So are you going to ignore my advice and waste a whole Season not seeing any other man but the one who quite patently does not want you?'

'There is still hope,' said Mira defiantly. 'He danced with me. And Drusilla can be such a bore. She has no intelligent conversation.'

'I haven't heard a word of intelligent conversation from you yet, miss. You are supposed to be flattering me and entertaining me.'

'But we are friends . . . I hope.'

39

'Try. You need practice. What operas have you seen? What plays? What gossip?'

'I have not been to the opera yet or the playhouse. Gossip? Mr. Brummell is fled to France, but everyone knows that. Lady Farnham ran off with her footman. Everyone knows that as well. I cannot find anything intriguing in the fact that a lady I don't know has run off with her footman. It is not very interesting.'

'Can you not flirt?'

She raised her fan, and those green eyes flashed a languishing look at him over the top. 'Like this?'

'Exactly like that, minx. I fear you were not made for fashionable society.'

She gave a little sigh. 'You have the right of it. I would rather be in the country. I love the changing seasons and the feeling of freedom one gets surrounded by woods and trees.'

He smiled. 'There is always Hyde Park. I will drive you there tomorrow at the fashionable hour—with your mother's permission, of course.'

'I should like that,' she said. 'Charles drives Drusilla there a lot.'

'I shall *not* take you if you are going to make sheep's eyes at Lord Charles!'

'I will be good,' said Mira meekly. 'I may as well use you to make myself fashionable.' She suddenly looked at him in consternation. 'How rude of me! I meant—'

'Ever practical, Miss Mira Markham. I know exactly what you mean. But you must pay attention to the other gentlemen about. Over there is young Mr. Danby. He danced the cotillion with you. He appeared charmed. You appeared indifferent. He comes from a good, solid, wealthy country family. He is near to you in age. This is his first Season as well. Should he ask you to dance again, do try to be a little more aware of him.'

Mira let out a gurgle of laughter. 'How like a governess you sound! Is there anyone else I should be getting my little hooks into?'

'There is Viscount Falling, the tall, thin man at the same table as your sister. He may look like a heron brooding over a pond, but he is kind and amiable. About my own age, which must seem ancient to you, but a good prospect. If you cannot have love, settle for an amiable man.'

'And what of yourself, my lord?' asked Mira curiously. 'All the gossip is that you have come to the Season to find yourself a bride.'

'Perhaps after tomorrow, when I consider I have paid you enough attention to set your steps on the right path, I shall turn my attention elsewhere.'

'Are . . . are you, too, attracted to my sister?'

'She is a handsome creature, I will allow, but spoiled. I would require more strength of character.'

Mira looked at him in amazement. She

reflected it was the first time she had heard any criticism of Drusilla at all. An odd loyalty to her sister prompted her to say defensively, 'She has been sadly indulged. But, you see, when one is so very beautiful, people do not worry whether one is unkind or . . . or . . .' She bit her lip, feeling that what had started out as a defense of her sister was degenerating into a criticism.

'Let us change the subject.' He looked at her empty plate. 'Would you like some more?'

'Yes, please, and may I have some more wine?'

'By all means.' He signaled to a waiter. 'Do you usually eat so much?'

'I have a healthy appetite. Besides, I have had nothing to eat since eleven o'clock this morning. There was tea and cake and things when we made our calls, but I was so nervous about this ball that I could not eat anything.'

'In future, Miss Mira, remember you are supposed to eat like a bird—and not a vulture either. Most ladies have plenty to eat before they go out for an evening to maintain the fiction.'

'It seems very rude to one's hosts to shun all the food they have arranged for us.'

'You will note the gentlemen more than make up for the deficiency. Now we have talked long enough to each other. You must engage the gentleman on your other side in conversation. He is Colonel Chalmers. You

42

will have a difficult time, as he lives and breathes army life.'

The marquess turned away, and Mira said to the elderly gentleman next to her, 'I am interested in finding out, sir, whether anyone ever really believed Napoleon would actually invade.'

'He is still a threat, and invasion may happen yet,' said the colonel. 'But you are too young to remember the fuss. We had tunnels dug into the cliffs at Dover so that several regiments could hide in there.'

'Why was that?'

'Don't you see,' he said eagerly, 'the idea was simple. If Boney invaded with his armies, then these regiments would stay hidden until the French troops moved inland. Then they would emerge from hiding and take them in the rear. And that's why we still have the cannon in Green Park, in case of invasion. Everyone used to drill every day in the parks. Then there was the threat of invasion from the sky.'

'I read about that,' said Mira, green eyes sparkling. 'The emperor had hundreds of balloons massed outside Boulogne.'

'But he decided to invade Russia,' cried the colonel, thumping the table in his enthusiasm.

The marquess, making polite conversation with the lady next to him, experienced amusement mixed with irritation when he realized Mira had temporarily forgotten his

43

existence as she discussed military matters with the colonel.

In fact, as supper finished, he had to try several times to catch her attention until she turned at last to him with a glowing face and said, 'Is not the colonel a famously interesting gentleman!'

'I am glad you enjoyed your conversation,' said the marquess. 'I shall escort you back to the ballroom.' As they left, the marquess heard the colonel say in a very loud voice, 'Now that is the prettiest and brightest girl I have ever met!'

Perhaps, he reflected, Mira's very unconventionality might gain her a place in society's notoriously flinty heart.

Mira entered the ballroom on his arm with a brand-new confidence, and then her heart soared as her mother approached her and said, 'Lord Charles has kindly asked my permission to take you driving tomorrow.' And before she could reply, her spirits were dashed when the marquess said firmly, 'I must insist that I have the prior claim. Miss Mira has already promised to accompany me, subject to your approval, Mrs. Markham.'

Even forthright Mira knew it would be in the worst of taste to protest. The marquess moved off, and Mira was immediately claimed by a gentleman for the next dance.

Between dances later that night Drusilla said to her mother, 'I am to drive with Lord

Charles tomorrow. I assume he asked your permission.'

'Oh, yes,' said Mrs. Markham vaguely, still mulling over the unexpected success of her younger daughter. 'Lord Charles asked at first to take Mira, but the Marquess of Grantley protested that he had asked her first, and so Lord Charles, when I told him, said he would escort you, Drusilla.'

Two angry spots of color burned in Drusilla's cheeks. 'Then I shall not go driving with Lord Charles, and so you may tell him, Mama. I do not like being second-best.'

'As to that, you must not be silly, Drusilla. Lord Charles is vastly taken with you. But he said to me that he felt he had been cruel in neglecting Mira, as he had always felt like an elder brother to her. He kindly volunteered to take her driving so that he could lecture her on how to go on.'

'In that case,' said Drusilla, mollified, 'I shall go with him. But you should warn Mira about making a cake of herself over the marquess. He is merely amusing himself with her, rather in the way that Charles was wont to do.'

Mrs. Markham said, 'That is possible. But she appears to have developed a freshness and charm that are somewhat appealing.'

For the first time in her young life, Drusilla began to fret about her own appearance. The feathers waving on her head restricted her movement, unlike Mira, with her garland of

45

flowers, who could spring through country dances, her head moving this way and that. She tried to copy Mira's liveliness of step but succeeded only in looking awkward.

She felt that Mira had somehow tricked her, had deliberately set out to outdo her, and plotted revenge.

*   *   *

The following day Drusilla's *amour propre* was further damaged by the servants, who had all learned of Mira's success at the ball, and Drusilla treated Betty, the maid, very harshly and threw the hairbrush at her, for Betty had dared to chatter on about how well Miss Mira had looked.

After she had dismissed the maid, Drusilla sat and thought. Mira deserved to be hurt for all her scheming, and the way to hurt Mira was through Charles. If she, Drusilla, could work Charles up to giving Mira a really blistering lecture, then Mira would be unhappy, and an unhappy Mira would lose that strange radiance she had so lately acquired.

And as Drusilla sat and thought about Mira, in Grosvenor Square, the marquess was also thinking about her. He was contrasting her with the lady present, who was everything Mira was not. His mother was visiting him, and the dowager marchioness had brought a 'young' friend with her, a certain Lady Jansen. Lady

46

Jansen was in her late twenties and a widow. She was calm and elegant, exquisitely gowned, and had no doubt been brought round, the marquess reflected cynically, to see if she could catch his eye. His mother was a tireless matchmaker on his behalf and constantly bemoaning her lack of grandchildren. But for the first time he had to admit he was interested. There was something very soothing in this lady of good sense, who was nearer him in years than the young misses of the Season. She had brown hair fashionably dressed in one of the new Roman styles, large pale blue eyes, a straight nose, and a small mouth. She had a generous bosom hoisted up high with a bodice, but then that was the fashion. Her husband, he learned, had died of cholera three years before.

'I saw you at the ball last night,' said Lady Jansen, 'paying court to all the pretty young girls.'

'Had I seen you, Lady Jansen,' said the marquess gallantly, 'I would have had eyes for no other.'

'That little chit with the green eyes is Mira Markham, is she not?'

'Yes.'

Lady Jansen gave a light laugh. 'I was surprised to see her being asked to dance even once after her rowdy behavior toward her sister. Do you know, my lord, that she pushed her sister into a goldfish pool?'

'I am aware of that episode.'

'I am surprised her mother did not send her packing to the country. She is ruining her beautiful sister's chances. The Markhams' vouchers to Almack's have been refused.'

'They will survive,' said the dowager marchioness. 'Those patronesses are becoming much too haughty. They are turning down so many people of note that if they are not careful, one will gain a cachet by being refused.'

'What did you think of Miss Mira?' pursued Lady Jansen.

'I found her very refreshing,' replied the marquess. 'In fact, I am to take her driving this afternoon.'

'Is that wise?' demanded his mother sharply. She was a small woman and rather fat but still had a commanding air. 'Mira Markham has disgraced herself, and I do not see why you should go out of your way to bring her into fashion.'

The marquess laughed. 'She is a hoyden, and she amuses me. I will tell you something, but you must promise not to tell anyone else.'

Both ladies swore they would not breathe a word.

He told them about Mira's acting as his tiger. Despite her shock and disapproval the dowager marchioness could not help laughing. 'I cannot but admire such courage in a girl,' she said when he had finished.

'Exactly,' said the marquess. 'So I am doing one more favor for her, and then I can forget about her.'

Lady Jansen, who had smiled indulgently throughout this account, thought busily behind the pleasant mask of her face. She had not expected competition. The marquess's mother had assured her that her son was heart-free. She shrewdly thought the marquess was intrigued with this minx, and if something was not done to put an end to his interest in Mira Markham, she might have no hope of the prize.

When she left she went to make calls and told the story of Mira's acting as tiger, swearing each lady to silence as she did so. The gossip spread outward, ever outward, until it seemed as if a heavy cloud pregnant with gossip and about to burst hung over the head of the unsuspecting Mira.

CHAPTER THREE

Lord Charles and the Marquess of Grantley were briefly left alone together in the drawing room while Mrs. Markham went to see if her daughters were ready. Mr. Markham had gone out to his club.

'I am glad of this opportunity to talk to you, Grantley,' began Lord Charles.

49

The marquess raised his thin eyebrows but said nothing.

'I am concerned for Mira.'

'Are you about to ask me my intentions?' asked the marquess haughtily.

'No!' Lord Charles looked horrified. 'I would not dream of being so impertinent. Besides, the whole idea is ridiculous. I merely caution you that Mira is inclined to be a trifle wild in her ways.'

'I have not noticed any wildness.' The marquess's voice was as cold as ice. 'If you have any complaint about Miss Mira, then I suggest you either tell her or tell her parents and refrain from criticizing a good friend of mine.'

Lord Charles flushed and opened his mouth to deliver an angry retort, but at that moment Mira and her sister came into the room.

Drusilla was calm and very beautiful in a carriage dress of blue velvet. Mira, in a carriage gown of gold velvet, was sparkling with excitement. The marquess stood up and bowed. 'Let us go, Miss Mira. We are fortunate. The day is relatively fine. I have a new carriage for you to inspect.'

They went outside, followed by Lord Charles and Drusilla. Outside stood the marquess's latest purchase, a high-perch phaeton with two black horses in tandem in front.

Holding the horses' heads was a small tiger.

'His name really is Jem,' said the marquess, and Mira giggled. Drusilla, listening to every word, wondered what was so funny about that.

As Mira and the marquess drove off, the marquess said, 'Are you looking forward to cutting a dash in the Park?'

'In this carriage,' said Mira appreciatively, 'one could cut a dash anywhere. What does one do in the Park?'

'One shows off. One drives round and nods to the fashionables, and then one goes home.'

'How dull.' Mira sighed. 'I have never even seen the river. I could be living in a village called the West End of London. To go outside it seems to be considered a sin.'

The sun was sparkling, and the air was warm. 'Would you like to see something of the rest of London?' asked the marquess.

'May I?'

'Of course. I shall show you the river first.'

Drusilla exclaimed to Lord Charles, 'Where are they going? That is not the way to the Park.'

'I do not care,' said Lord Charles, who was still smarting over the marquess's put-down.

Mira had temporarily forgotten about Lord Charles. She saw the River Thames from Westminster Bridge. She saw the Temple Bar, and then they bowled along Fleet Street and up Ludgate Hill past the mercers' shops to St. Paul's Cathedral. When the marquess reminded her that her drive in the Park would be expected to be over and that she should return, she heaved a sigh of disappointment.

'So soon? Do you go to the opera tonight. my lord?'

'Yes, my chuck. Catalini is singing. I hope you will be able to hear her above the chatter of society.'

Mira glanced up at him shyly. 'Will you dance with me at the opera ball?'

He hesitated. He had not intended to attend the ball after the opera. 'I am sorry,' she said quickly. 'That was forward of me. How can you find a bride if I keep making demands on you?'

'I am sure a dance with you will not stop me from looking at other pretty ladies,' said the marquess. 'Very well. One dance. But you must try to attract some beaux.'

'I think if I cannot marry Charles, then I would rather not be married at all,' said Mira.

'May I point out to you again that you are not in love with Lord Charles.'

'How can you tell?'

'Love is not all gladness and happiness, my innocent; it can be a type of suffering. Were you in love with Lord Charles, you would have gone to the Park, longing for every moment you could have a sight of him, hoping against hope that he would notice you or that my presence would make him jealous.'

'Then you have been in love?'

'At my great age it would be a miracle had I not been.'

Mira wanted to ask him whether he had actually been in love with his wife, something she had quickly learned in her short stay in London was highly unusual. Marriage was a trade, your fortune to match my fortune, your lands to join my lands. Love had little to do with it. He was not *that* old, about somewhere in his early thirties, or so she had overheard her mother saying.

They drove back in amicable silence. He was just helping her down from the carriage when the Markhams' butler approached them. 'If you would be so good as to step upstairs to the drawing room, my lord. My master is desirous of a word with you.'

'Now what's this about?' the marquess asked Mira.

'Perhaps Drusilla, who was behind us, saw us driving in the opposite direction of the Park and reported it to Papa.'

His face cleared. 'Oh, that is of no moment. There is nothing shameful about driving a lady about London in an open carriage. We have done nothing we ought not to do.'

But when he walked into the drawing room behind Mira, he stared about him, suddenly worried. Drusilla was there, as was Lord Charles. Lord Charles was looking stern, and Drusilla had an air of gleeful anticipation. Mr. and Mrs. Markham had stern faces.

'Pray be seated, my lord,' said Mr. Markham. 'We have just received some distressing news.'

'If it is distressing news, I prefer to stand in order to hear it.'

'As you will. We have received a report that you went on a curricle race to Sands Hill and that Mira here, dressed in boy's clothes, acted as your tiger.'

Before Mira could speak, the marquess said with chilly haughtiness, 'And you believed this?'

'My lord, I could not do else. It was a most reliable source.'

'Namely?'

'Mrs. Gardener.'

A look of contemptuous amusement crossed the marquess's handsome face. 'Mrs. Gardener is the most malicious gossip in London.' He assumed an air of patient reason, like a weary parent talking to slightly backward children. 'My attentions to Miss Mira have, you must be aware, caused a certain amount of jealousy. I have never heard a more ridiculous story.'

He received help from an unexpected quarter. Drusilla, sure now that the story was all lies, was still smarting over Mrs. Gardener's description of how she, Drusilla, had been humiliated at the ball by assuming the marquess wished to dance with her when the invitation was for Mira.

'*I* never believed a word of it,' she said.

'But it is such an elaborate story,' said Mr. Markham, still plainly puzzled. He swung round to Mira. 'Is there any truth in this rumor?'

'I wish there were,' said Mira ruefully, and the marquess could not help but admire her acting ability. 'I should like that above all things, to masquerade as a tiger. But did you go on a race, my lord?'

'Yes, Miss Mira, and with a most recalcitrant tiger. My own had disappeared, and this urchin approached me in Grosvenor Square and offered his services. He was competent enough, but he brawled in the inn yard with one of the other tigers, and I had to cuff his ears.' He turned to Mr. Markham. 'If you ask any of the gentlemen who were on that race with me, you will find they will support my story of the fighting tiger. Can you imagine your daughter fighting in an inn yard?'

Mr. Markham gave a reluctant smile. 'My apologies. I should not have believed such a tale.'

'But where did you go this afternoon?' demanded Drusilla. 'We did not see you in the Park.'

'I drove Miss Mira to Westminster Bridge instead to look at the river, a harmless occupation and quite conventional. Now I would like to take my leave.' Haughty disdain was back on the marquess's face, alarming Mr. and Mrs. Markham, who had no wish to alienate this lord, who had been so kind as to bring the unruly Mira into fashion.

'Please, my lord,' said Mr. Markham, 'you must understand our concern. The story seems fantastic now, but at the time it had the ring of truth because it was just the sort of thing Mira might once have done.'

Mrs. Markham felt that things were getting worse and that her husband was being unusually clumsy in even suggesting that Mira could be a hoyden.

The marquess appeared to relent. 'I shall see you all at the opera tonight. I have promised Miss Mira a dance.'

But when he left them and reached the street, his face was grim and set. He drove straight to his mother's. The dowager marchioness preferred to live in a little town house of her own in South Audley Street, claiming that she felt lost in the large family mansion in Grosvenor Square.

He mounted the stairs and entered his mother's drawing room. She had been sleeping in an armchair by the fireplace, but came awake with a start when he marched into the room. He tossed his hat into a corner and sat down opposite her.

'Mama, that Gardener female saw fit to call on the Markhams and regale them with the story of Miss Mira being my tiger. It could have originated only from you or Lady Jansen.'

His mother sat up straight, blinking in alarm. 'It was not I!' she exclaimed. 'Would I, your mother, spread such a story about? Do you think I want you to marry a rowdy little chit like this Mira? And that is what you may have to do if this is believed.'

'I scotched it. But that means that Lady Jansen is the culprit.'

'Oh, but she is such a dear lady and the soul of discretion. I thought she would make you the ideal wife. No, no, one of the servants must have been listening at the door.'

'Which untrustworthy servant would that be?'

'I do not know. John, the footman? But he has been with you some years now, and your butler is above reproach.'

'Then we come back to Lady Jansen. I do not wish you to have anything further to do with that woman, nor do I wish you to introduce me to any more females. Should I choose to marry again, then I am perfectly capable of finding my own bride.'

'To be sure,' said his mother weakly, 'I was only trying to help.'

'Don't!'

The dowager marchioness looked sulky. 'Your dear father would never have spoken to me in such a way. But, yes, yes, when Lady Jansen calls, I will not admit her.'

*   *   *

Lady Jansen prepared herself with great care for the opera that night. She felt sure the marquess would be there. The gossip she had spread would already be working. Little Mira Markham would be in such disgrace now that her parents, in order to protect the reputation of the elder, beautiful daughter, would be forced to return Mira to the country. She thought constantly of the marquess. He had looked on her with approval. When his mother had at first slyly suggested she might be a suitable bride for her son, she had been interested, but only because of the marquess's wealth and title. But when she had met him, she had realized that here was the man of her dreams. Her passionate and voluptuous nature, which had never been allowed to blossom in an arranged marriage or among the strict rules and taboos and shibboleths of London society, smoldered away dangerously. She had never taken a lover as had some other widows.

Her opera gown of gold tissue, she thought, lent her a stately but seductive air. She turned this way and that before the long glass, trying to shrug off a bright little image of Mira. The girl was positively plain with those Slavic cheekbones.

She summoned her companion, one of those sad, indigent females who eke out an existence chaperoning such as Lady Jansen. Her box, Lady Jansen knew, faced that of the marquess across the opera house. She was sure her golden gown and diamond tiara would catch his eye.

As she had little interest in the music and liked to make an entrance, she planned to arrive at the first interval, unaware that her poor companion was looking forward so much to hearing Catalini sing and that music was the one consolation in her rather miserable existence. Her name was Mrs. Anderson, the Mrs. being a courtesy title, for Mrs. Anderson was in her forties and had never married, the fate of so many of little looks and less dowry.

That Mrs. Anderson, who was small and mousy, was capable of hate would have surprised Lady Jansen very much, but Mrs. Anderson did hate her employer for the many little indignities and cruelties she was subjected to. She was wearing a gown that Lady Jansen had grown tired of. It was a merino gown of red-and-white stripes, which Mrs. Anderson considered vulgar but wore because the material was good, and also it was warm.

Mrs. Anderson knew all about Lady Jansen's hope of snaring this marquess and had been with her on calls that day when she had set out to ruin the reputation of some chit called Mira Markham. Mrs. Anderson did hope that Mira Markham had somehow survived the damage done to her reputation, for she was eager to see this spirited girl who dressed as a boy and went on races. Mrs. Anderson admired spirit, having very little of that commodity herself.

They arrived at the opera house exactly in time for the first interval. Mrs. Anderson sat down quietly at the back of the box, blinking a little in the glare of lights from the huge chandelier that hung in the middle of the theater.

Lady Jansen sat waiting impatiently for callers. After a few moments she took out a pair of opera glasses and leveled them on the marquess's box. It was empty. She swung it along the boxes and then stiffened. The marquess was in the Markhams' box. She could just make out his golden head above the press of men crowding around the Markham sisters. They all seemed to be laughing a lot.

She slowly lowered the glasses at the end of the interval, for as the callers left, she could see Mira quite clearly. What had happened? Then she sat back and forced herself to be patient. The gossip, which usually spread like wildfire, had obviously not reached the Markham parents yet.

The opera began again, and she fidgeted impatiently while little Mrs. Anderson gave her soul up to the music.

The next interval was no better. This time she saw the marquess rise and leave his box only to reappear in the Markhams' box. She swung her glasses angrily about the other boxes until she located that famous gossip, Mrs. Gardener. Good. It was only a matter of time.

For his part the marquess had made a very amusing story about the 'lie' about himself and Mira. He then suggested to the other callers in the Markhams' box that they all invent some really horrendous lie about Mrs. Gardener and spread it about, and the laughter rose loudly when Mira offered that they suggest that Mrs. Gardener's magnificent head of white hair was actually a wig and dare people to take tugs at it.

And all the while Mira laughed and joked, she had a dismal awareness that she was telling lies. Her green eyes flew from time to time to the marquess's face, seeking reassurance, but he looked blandly back, and she did not know that he was well aware that the real source of the gossip was sitting in the opera house at that very moment.

Lady Jansen fantasized about the marquess all through the last act. He had not called at her box because he did not know she was present, or so she persuaded herself. She should have arrived at the beginning of the performance. But there was always the opera ball. He would ask her to dance. She would float in his arms. She would fascinate him with her conversation, surely so mature and wise compared to that of Mira Markham. Like most rather stupid, humorless, and selfish people, Lady Jansen prided herself on her own wisdom and sound good sense. Men did not like a bluestocking, admittedly, but she was firmly convinced that a good figure and gentlewomanly wisdom were a nigh irresistible combination.

She was relieved when the 'tiresome' performance was over and one of the finest voices in the whole of Britain and Europe was finally silent.

Ordering Mrs. Anderson curtly to carry her fan and shawl, she made her way to the ballroom.

To her annoyance the first dance was claimed by some elderly colonel who bored her with military matters when they met during the figure of the dance. During the promenade she reminded him gently that talk of wars and battles was not suitable for gentle ears, to which the elderly colonel glared at her and said, 'Forgot. Beg pardon. Trouble is, I was talking to a vastly intelligent girl the other night, Miss Mira Markham. Forgot the rest of you were dim as parish lamps.'

With irritation coloring her cheeks Lady Jansen sat down again. But her heart surged as the marquess approached her and asked her to dance. And it was the waltz. For a few moments she was so wrapped up in rapturous dreams of being the next Marchioness of Grantley that it was with a start she realized he was actually talking to her. 'Why did you spread that gossip about Mira Markham?' he was asking.

Her eyes flickered uneasily. Useless to deny it. Mrs. Gardener would say firmly that she had been the source. She manufactured a light laugh. 'It was too amusing an on-dit, my lord, and Mira Markham has already been socially damned.'

'I had your word you would not gossip,' he said roundly. 'Fortunately no one believes the gossip. My mother wishes you to cease calling on her. You nearly ruined the reputation of one young lady.'

She could not think what to say. She felt absolutely wretched. Misery made her movements wooden. He did not promenade with her, but as soon as the waltz was finished turned and walked abruptly away.

Then she found herself confronted by a very angry Mrs. Gardener. 'How cruel of you to tell me such lies,' cried Mrs. Gardener in her shrill, piercing voice. And then over her shoulder Lady Jansen saw that the Dowager Marchioness of Grantley had arrived.

'I did not lie,' she said. 'Come with me and hear the truth from his own mother.' Not only did Mrs. Gardener follow her to where the marchioness sat but a curious little group of fellow gossipmongers tagged along as well.

Lady Jansen confronted the elderly dowager marchioness. 'Do tell Mrs. Gardener, dear Marchioness, that your son did admit to going on a curricle race with Mira Markham as his tiger.'

It was between dances. Her voice carried. Suddenly it seemed as if everyone was listening avidly. The dowager's old voice was as clear as a bell. 'Nonsense,' she said. 'I have never heard such a farrago of lies. Be off with you. Our friendship is at an end.' She looked about her and shook her head. 'Poor woman. It's the laudanum, you know. Addles the wits.'

Mrs. Anderson, standing behind her employer, felt a surge of pure glee. Heads were bent, whispering and whispering. Mira Markham was beginning to appear in the eyes of society as a fascinating figure. After all, she was someone who had excited enough jealousy in Lady Jansen's bosom to make that normally staid lady tell terrible lies about her. Debutantes eyed Mira's hitherto despised cheekbones and decided to throw away their wax pads and perhaps go on the fashionable diet of steak, potatoes, and vinegar.

The marquess was beginning to feel sorry for Lady Jansen. He felt he had been too hard on her. It had, after all, been a delicious piece of gossip that Lady Jansen had innocently repeated. All society gossiped, and it was his own fault for having told his mother about Mira in front of a lady to whom he had been newly introduced. That Lady Jansen had used the gossip to try to ruin Mira was a Gothic idea. One had only to look at her. Such a respectable and sensible lady could not stoop to such depths. And much as the marquess,

64

like everyone else, despised Mrs. Gardener, it was still very unfair to damn the woman so. After a shamed Lady Jansen had resumed her seat, the marquess joined his mother. 'I fear I have been too harsh on Lady Jansen. I presented her with an irresistible piece of gossip.'

'Well, you have shamed her in public, and so have I,' said his mother, 'and I do not feel comfortable about it at all.'

The marquess made up his mind. 'I shall take her in to supper and look so well pleased with her that society will begin to think it was all a joke.'

Mira danced with partner after partner but never with either Charles or the marquess. The one would have enchanted her and the other reassured her, she thought, feeling suddenly friendless. But the marquess would no doubt take her up for the supper dance, and then they would eat together and chat away, and she would bask in the envy of less fortunate debutantes and be able to forget about Charles for just a little.

When the supper dance was announced, she waited hopefully, but Charles asked Drusilla, and to her amazement the marquess approached that stately lady whom the gossipmongers had told her had been the real source of the gossip against her, that Lady Jansen, and took her onto the floor. She forced a smile on her face when elderly Colonel

Chalmers bowed before her. 'I don't see why the young fellow should have all the fun,' he said. Mira liked the colonel and so forced herself to dance prettily and to entertain the old boy so well during supper that she succeeded in looking as if she did not have a care in the world.

The marquess, for his part, was enjoying the undemanding company of a grateful Lady Jansen. She was experienced enough to draw him out and get him to talk about himself and his estates. She appeared to have a great knowledge of agriculture, a subject she actually loathed but quickly divined was close to the marquess's heart. The marquess gallantly apologized for having been so rude to her, saying that he should have known a lady of such good nature and good sense would never deliberately set out to destroy the reputation of a 'little girl' like Mira.

But the evening for Mira was not a total disaster, for Charles said he had secured permission to take her driving. She barely slept that night, wrapped up in rosy dreams of soon being alone with Charles as in the old days.

How long the next day seemed before that precious drive! Gentlemen she had danced with the night before called to pay their respects.

She fussed over her dress and kept running to the window to look anxiously at the sky, which was cloudy and overcast. An irritating little wind was blowing straw along the street.

When it was time to descend to the drawing room, she felt quite exhausted with lack of sleep and the effort of trying on one outfit after the other. Charles looked incredibly remote and handsome. She could feel her newfound confidence ebbing. She tried to remember what the marquess had said about moral courage and not focus on petty things, like how the damp air would make her wretched hair even more frizzy.

Charles talked politely of this and that as he drove her to the Park. She tried to tease him in the old way, but he appeared not to hear what she was saying or he chose not to. When they reached the Park, he bowed to various acquaintances and friends, and Mira fell silent. But when they were making the round for the second time, he said, 'The reason I asked you to come with me, Mira, is because I wish to talk to you privately.'

Her mercurial spirits soared. She turned shining eyes up to his face. 'Oh, and I have longed to be private with you, dear Charles,' she said.

But he went on in a flat, even voice. 'The fact is this, Mira: I am about to propose marriage to Drusilla. I worship her and can think of no greater happiness in life than that she should be my bride.'

A spot of rain fell on Mira's cheek. It felt like a tear. She found her voice. 'I hope you will be very happy, Charles.'

'I hope so, too. Now your sister is a gentle creature, delicate as a flower. She has told me how worried she is about your behavior. You must try to be supportive to her, Mira, and put your hoydenish ways behind you. There is still a boldness about you that can do nothing but displease. I am sure you will not mind my speaking to you like this, for I have always regarded myself as an older brother to you. Try for a little more maidenly modesty. And do not take the flattering attentions of Grantley too seriously. He was merely amusing himself by bringing you back into fashion. I notice he did not dance with you last night. There are plenty of young men at the Season more of your age.'

'The marquess is not much older than you, Charles.' Mira bit her lip to fight back the tears.

'But too worldly and experienced and sophisticated a man for a child like you, Mira. It is threatening rain. So I am soon to be your brother-in-law, Mira. Think of that!'

And Mira did think of it all the way home as her poor head ached and the alien and hostile world of London lay all about her. She realized that despite Charles's interest in Drusilla, she had hoped and dreamed that he would marry *her*. Before they reached home, she said in a small voice, 'I cannot see Drusilla as an army bride, Charles.'

He smiled complacently. 'Nor I. Such a

gentle flower must not be bruised by a barracks life. I am selling out.'

Perhaps it was that simple statement that made Mira suddenly realize how ridiculous her dreams had been, for Charles had loved his life in the army, and here he was, prepared to sacrifice everything for the love of Drusilla.

She thanked him politely for the drive. He said he would not accompany her indoors but would probably see her on the following day after he had proposed to Drusilla—and, hopefully, he said with a shadow of his former boyish grin, been accepted.

Mira curtsied low and then ran up the steps. She went straight to her room, slumped in an armchair by the window, and stared unseeingly in front of her. She wished now that the gossip about her had stuck and that she had been banished to the country. There she could ride and go on walks and talk to the townspeople.

They were to go to the playhouse that evening. Mira knew that Charles would have asked her parents' permission to call the following day to propose to Drusilla and that they would talk of little else during the evening, and so she roused herself to call the maid and say she had a headache. Then she allowed the maid to undress her and put her to bed.

But she lay awake, listening to the sounds of the house and then the sounds of departure. When she heard the family carriage drive off, she roused herself from bed. She manufactured a dummy of herself from the bolster, a cushion, and a nightcap. She had sworn never to wear masculine clothes again, but she was hurting badly and craved the marquess's comfort and advice. She would change and go round to Grosvenor Square and perhaps catch him as he was leaving for the evening.

Somehow, to her, her masculine dress did not feel at all disgraceful in the evening, for London had that hectic nighttime feeling it always had in the West End as society set out to drink and dance and gamble the night away.

She had expected him to be there, perhaps just getting into his carriage or walking out to his club, but his house had a shuttered air. She walked slowly round to the mews at the back and shoving her hands in her pockets approached a loitering groom and asked him which was the marquess's carriage. 'Several of them,' said the groom. 'Taken the closed one out tonight to the playhouse.'

Mira ambled off, feeling more miserable than ever. If she had gone to the playhouse with her family, then she might have had the opportunity of a few words with him. Still, she might be able to see him after the performance. She began to walk in the direction of Drury Lane.

She walked up and down the waiting carriages until she recognized the marquess's tiger, Jem. He was lounging against a closed carriage, talking to a coachman. Mira crept around the far side of the carriage and opened the door. She crawled inside and gently closed the door behind her, wrapped a huge bearskin carriage rug about her, and lay on the floor. The time dragged on. There was the play, and after the play there would be a farce or a harlequinade.

The misery of the day overcame her, and she closed her eyes and fell asleep.

*　　　*　　　*

The marquess entered his carriage and then started in surprise as his foot struck the bearskin rug on the floor and it emitted a startled yelp. He pulled it aside, and in the flickering light of a parish lamp outside the carriage, he saw the white face of Mira Markham staring up at him.

'What are you about?' he growled. 'Are you hell-bent on ruining yourself?'

Mira's eyes filled with tears. 'I am so miserable.'

'For heaven's sake. Get out if you can without being seen, and wait for me at the corner.'

He waited impatiently until Mira had quietly crept out and shut the door behind her, and then he opened the trap in the roof with his sword stick and called to his coachman. 'I have decided to walk. Take the carriage home.'

'Raining again, my lord,' called the coachman.

'Nonetheless I will walk.'

He joined Mira at the end of the street and put a hand on her shoulder. 'We'll find somewhere out of the rain where we can talk. I hope you have a good explanation for this scandalous behavior. Will your parents or the servants not miss you?'

'I said I had a headache, my lord, and left a dummy in my bed. They will not notice.'

'Thank goodness for small mercies. Just let us hope no one recognized you. Pull your hat down more over your face.'

Home-going carriages from the playhouse passed them. Lady Jansen looked out, recognized the marquess a little ahead walking in the rain, and debated whether to call to her coachman to stop and then offer him a lift. But her eyes sharpened as she saw the 'boy' walking next to him. Surely there was something familiar about that lithe figure. The couple walked under a lamp as her carriage came alongside them. For a brief moment Mira turned her face up to the marquess's, and Lady Jansen recognized her.

She leaned back in her seat and fanned herself vigorously. It was all too plain to her that the marquess was having an affair with the chit. Why else would he walk about London with her dressed as a boy? She must think what to do. She could not risk ridicule again. And the marquess had not proposed to Mira Markham, so that underlined the fact that his intentions were highly dishonorable.

There was yet hope . . . if she plotted and planned carefully.

CHAPTER FOUR

'Here, I think,' said the marquess, entering a coffeehouse in the Strand. Mira crunched across the discarded oyster shells on the sawdust-covered floor and followed him to a table in a shadowy corner.

The marquess ordered coffee for both of them. His eyes looked black behind the stump of a candle that burned in its flat stick on the tabletop between them.

'Now, Miss Mira,' he said, 'begin at the beginning and go on to the end.'

'Charles took me driving today.'

There was a silence.

'Go on,' prompted the marquess gently.

'He told me he is to propose to Drusilla tomorrow. He told me to mend my ways. Worse than that—'

'There's worse?'

'Yes, he loves Drusilla so much that he is selling out. He will probably buy a property near us in the country, and he will be my brother-in-law.'

'My opinion,' said the marquess, 'is that Lord Charles has probably grown and changed since the days of your childhood into a rather pompous man. If you keep on searching for the easygoing companion of your youth, you will continue to be disappointed.'

'It is so very hard to take,' said Mira in a low voice. 'I know I am behaving disgracefully, but I had to talk to *someone*.'

The great Marquess of Grantley gave a wry smile. He was not used to hearing himself described as 'someone'.

'You are going to have to be very brave,' he said, 'and put it all behind you and concentrate on trying to enjoy this Season. If you try very hard, pretence will soon become reality.'

'Another thing disturbs me,' said Mira. 'I did not like lying to my parents or ridiculing Mrs. Gardener. I first had a feeling that such a tattle-tale deserved it, but she only spoke the truth as given to her by that Lady Jansen.'

'I am afraid the fault was really all mine.' The marquess poured more coffee. 'I told the story of our adventure to amuse my mother. Lady Jansen was present. I should have known it was too good a piece of gossip to remain unspread. I am sorry I had to lie and encourage you to lie as well, but your reputation was at stake.'

'I think Lady Jansen is a despicable woman,' said Mira fiercely, 'and yet you took her in to supper and appeared well pleased with her.'

'I was, and I have forgiven her,' said the marquess. 'She is a lady of good sense.'

'I do not think spreading dangerous and malicious gossip a sign of good sense!'

'Your sex *will* gossip.'

'Not I! If you told me not to tell anyone something, then I would not!'

'You are not typical of your sex, my chuck. Young society ladies do not venture out at night dressed as boys.'

'Well, you cannot know that,' retorted Mira, all mad reason. She waved an expansive arm. 'This coffeehouse could be full of them.'

'That I doubt, Miss Mira. You are an original. Are you sure you can return home without being observed?'

She tugged a large key out of her pocket. 'I took the spare key to the back door when I left.'

'When you finish your coffee, I suggest I take you home. Do you feel better?'

'Somewhat. Not much. If I were in the country, I would take my mare, Sally, out of the stables and ride and ride.'

He hesitated and then said, 'If you are very sure your absence will not be discovered, I could lend you a mount, and we could go for a night ride.'

Those green eyes sparkled. 'I would like that above all things.'

'Then I rely on you to keep quiet about it.'

Mira surveyed him with a quaint haughtiness. 'You do not need to tell *me* to keep quiet. I have my virtues, my lord.'

His eyes shone with amusement. 'Are you a very good rider?'

'I am accounted so. There is no need to find me a quiet lady's mount.'

'Then we will take some exercise. You will need to walk home with me while I change into riding clothes. Fortunately for you I am an indulgent master and do not have my servants waiting up for me—the house servants, that is. I will need to rouse the head groom to saddle up for us.

London had changed back to an exciting and wonderful place in Mira's eyes as they walked together through the rain-washed streets. The rain had ceased to fall, and a tiny moon, a hunter's moon, was riding high above the jumbled chimney pots.

When they reached his house in Grosvenor Square, he produced a door key, opened the door, and ushered her in. 'You had best come upstairs with me,' he said. 'I had a young nephew staying here, and he has left some of his clothes. I may be able to find something to fit you more suitable for riding than what you have on. Your clothes are still damp.'

He was amused to sense that innocent Mira saw nothing odd about being unchaperoned in his home. He led her into a bedchamber, lit the lamps, and searched in a large press in the corner and then threw a riding outfit on the bed. 'Change into that and meet me downstairs.'

Mira changed into the clothes after stripping off and rubbing herself vigorously with a towel. She put on the clothes, which fitted her well, plaited her frizzy hair, and taking a bone pin from the pocket of the damp coat she had discarded, skewered the plait on top of her head and then put a curly brimmed beaver on top of it. She surveyed herself in the glass. She had tied a cravat in a simple style. She thought she looked the very picture of a young gentleman.

When she went down to the hall, he was changed and waiting. 'Good,' he said, looking her up and down.

They walked round to the mews, where he roused the groom and asked for two horses to be saddled up.

Soon they were riding together sedately out of Grosvenor Square. 'Where to?' called Mira.

'The parks are closed. We take the Great West Road again. Go easily on the gravel, and we will swing away across country after Knightsbridge. Look out for footpads.'

After Knightsbridge they set out across the open fields. Then he called, 'Now!' and they both spurred their horses.

Mira felt the magnificent Arab he had lent her surge under her. Under the moon they rode with the wind whistling in their ears. Mira felt she could ride forever. London was in the distance, London with its peculiar society and its grim laws, London with heartless Charles.

He finally slowed to a canter and then a trot, reining in finally on top of a rise. A pale dawn was spreading across the sky, and the first birds were beginning to twitter.

'Better?' he asked.

'Much better,' said Mira, leaning forward and patting the horse's neck.

'We had better return. Your servants will soon be awake.'

As they rode easily back to London, he talked of his home in the country, of improvements to the land, and then said, 'I may decide to return and forgo the rest of the Season.'

'Wait a little longer,' said Mira. 'I need your help a little longer.'

He had dismounted. He reached up and lifted her down from the saddle. She was pressed against his chest. He suddenly felt a spurt of anger at her sheer indifference to his masculinity, and before he could stop himself, he kissed her full on the mouth. Sheer shock kept her still until he released her.

'That is to teach you a lesson,' he said, standing back. 'Be careful in future of treating men as friends. London can be a wicked place.'

Mira backed away from him, her hand to her mouth. 'So I have found out,' she whispered. She turned and ran away. He stood for a long moment, hearing the clatter of her feet on the cobbles, and then he shrugged and tried to put her out of his mind, tried not to tell himself that he had behaved cruelly and badly. He could still taste her lips, young and sweet and full. He swore under his breath and called loudly for his groom.

*   *   *

Mira managed to gain the privacy of her room, unobserved. She carefully took off the clothes he had given her, wondering in a numb sort of way if she would ever have the courage to return them to him or to face him again. She washed and changed into her nightdress and lay down on the bed after having taken the dummy out. She lay on her back, very still, and stared up at the bed canopy. The sounds of morning London filtered into the room, carriages, street cries, footsteps, dusters flapping from windows as the maids went about their work, and the occasional clatter of an iron hoop, bowled along the pavement by a child.

That kiss had changed everything. Unlike Sleeping Beauty the kiss had awakened her to a difficult world of reality. A child had slipped out to meet the marquess the night before, and a woman had returned. This was the day Charles was coming to propose to Drusilla, and she felt . . . nothing. She turned abruptly over on her side and fell asleep, not waking until two in the afternoon, when she was roused by the maid, who told her coyly that she had to put one of her best gowns on and make herself ready for a family celebration.

When she entered the drawing room, she was not at first aware of Charles and Drusilla standing holding hands in front of the fireplace but of her father. Mr. Markham was surveying her with an odd half-questioning, half-anxious look in his eyes.

'Wish your sister every happiness,' said Mrs. Markham. 'She and Charles are to wed.'

Mira went forward and kissed Drusilla on the cheek. 'I hope you will be very happy.' She then curtsied to Charles. 'It is a pleasure to welcome you as a member of the family.'

It was prettily done, but Mira was still turning over the events of the night before in her mind and so was not aware of Drusilla's startled and petulant look of surprise. Drusilla had been looking forward so much to scoring over Mira that Mira's calm acceptance of her engagement took all the excitement out of it, and for the first time Drusilla began to wonder uneasily if she really wanted to be married to Charles. And what had happened to little Mira, accepting a glass of champagne and looking very much the mistress of herself and her emotions?

Charles talked about how he planned to sell out of the army and discussed a 'tidy property' near their own in the country that he had his eye on. And Mira, drinking and listening to him, could no longer see him with the eyes of love. He seemed a staid man, middle-aged before his time, and rather pompous.

'We are to attend the Freemonts' ball in Kensington tonight,' said Mrs. Markham with satisfaction, for to have one daughter engaged so early in the Season was a triumph, and although the announcement would not be in the newspapers until the following morning, Mrs. Markham intended that people should know of her triumph as soon as possible.

Mira hoped the marquess would not be at the ball. He had suddenly become a stranger to her, an incalculable man rather than a friend. But he had given her good advice, and she would take it. If she married someone, say, like young Mr. Danby, then she would have an establishment of her own, her own horses and dogs, and children. Children! She had not thought of children before. If she had children, she could teach them to ride. If she had girls, she would not produce another Mira. She would train a daughter to be a young miss from the beginning. And a son? Her eyes grew misty with dreams.

Charles, glancing at her, was arrested by the transformed glow on her face. How odd Mira was, he reflected. He had always accepted the Markham family idea that Mira was the plain one, and yet she seemed to have a strange,

81

almost fey beauty. He found himself reluctantly remembering her courage and humor. Mira would never have expected you to leave the army, said a treacherous little voice in his head. He turned quickly and looked down at the beauty that was Drusilla Markham. He would be the envy of every man in London.

*　　*　　*

The marquess took Lady Jansen out for a drive that afternoon. The fact that he found her company unexciting and undemanding soothed his guilty soul. Damn Mira and her wild, unconventional ways. He realized his companion was asking him whether he meant to attend the ball in Kensington that night. Damn Mira again! She would be there, and how on earth was he going to approach her? He had, he admitted to himself ruefully, enjoyed her easygoing friendship, and now he had shattered that.

'You have not replied.' admonished Lady Jansen, tapping his arm playfully with her fan.

'I am sorry. I was daydreaming. Yes, I will be there.'

'And Miss Mira?'

He gave her a sharp glance. 'I believe so. Why do you ask?'

'I wondered whether I ought to beg her forgiveness.'

82

His face cleared. He found himself liking her very much.

'I do not think that at all necessary. It is better the matter be forgotten.'

She gave a little laugh. 'Nonetheless I should never have repeated such a story. You may trust me now. I could not bear such shame again.'

'As I said, it is forgotten. Miss Mira will no doubt soon be engaged to a fellow of her own age and pursuits.'

Lady Jansen tried to feel comforted by that remark, but she kept seeing Mira's bright face turned up to his under the parish light in Drury Lane. If only she could find some hard proof of the marquess's liaison with this girl, then Mira would soon be sent out of London in disgrace, never to be heard of again.

When the marquess escorted her home, she rested for an hour on her bed without sleeping, thinking all the time of how to obtain the necessary proof. And then she remembered her friend, Mrs. Jackson, a jealous woman who became convinced her husband was having an affair. Most married society women suspected their husbands kept mistresses but would not dream of raising the subject or doing anything about it. But Mrs. Jackson loved her husband, a rare state of affairs. She had employed a retired Bow Street Runner by the name of Diggs. That was it, Diggs. Lady Jansen rang the bell, rose, and went to the writing desk next door in her boudoir. She scribbled a note to Mrs. Jackson, folded it, sanded it, and sent the footman, who answered the summons of the bell, to go directly to Mrs. Jackson's with it and wait for a reply.

By the time she set out for the ball, she had secured the address of the retired Runner. At the ball, when the marquess approached her first and led her onto the floor, the better side of her nature decided to forget about the ex-Runner. If she just went on the way she was going and remained uncomplicated and friendly, she was sure the marquess would propose marriage to her.

But she was becoming rapidly obsessed with the marquess, with his splendid figure, his golden hair, his strong face, and the way those gray eyes could look down into her own so intently when she said something to catch his attention. So her feelings when Mira Markham walked into the ballroom were of rage and sick, poisonous jealousy. Some might say that Mira was not a beauty, that her cheekbones were too high, her hair too frizzy, but she had youth and a gracefulness of movement.

Mr. Danby, asking Mira to dance, was charmed to receive her full attention this time. As they walked after the dance, she talked easily of horses and dogs and country pursuits so dear to his own heart. He did not feel awkward with her or feel he had to pay her extravagant compliments. He was fascinated by those green eyes of hers and loved to see them sparkle with laughter. He had discussed his interest in Mira with his mother, who had said doubtfully that although the girl had initially disgraced herself, she had behaved prettily ever since. The Markhams were very wealthy, and Mrs. Danby was certainly not going to steer her only son away from a rich dowry.

Mr. Danby was an engaging-looking young man with curly black hair, a rather snub nose, and a pleasant smile. 'What a good couple they make,' remarked Lady Jansen to the marquess. The marquess agreed but privately thought Mira was too high-spirited and intelligent for a callow youth such as Danby, and the fact that he had recommended Danby as a suitable suitor to Mira did not help his temper.

He had been taken aback by Mira's self-possession. He had expected her to look at him reproachfully or blush or show some sign of maidenly distress, but her eyes had met his across the ballroom, clear and unafraid, and she had dropped a brief curtsy in his direction before turning back to her partner.

Perhaps if he had left her to the attentions of Mr. Danby, Lady Jansen would have forgotten about employing Diggs. But something persuaded the marquess that he had to apologize or explain his behavior, and so he joined Mira after the promenade and asked her to save the supper dance for him.

This Lady Jansen did not know at the time, but as soon as the supper dance was announced and she looked across at the marquess with a smile of anticipation, it was to see him cross to Mira's side and then lead her into the steps of the waltz.

They danced well together. People were remarking on how beautifully Mira Markham danced. As their bodies weaved about each other, the filmy stuff of Mira's gown floating out around her, Lady Jansen saw them in bed together, writhing in bed together, and wondered what society would think of this oh-so-innocent miss if society could but know. She would find Diggs the next day and pay him what he required to expose the guilty couple. A shamed Mira would be sent away, and then the field would be open to her.

The marquess said in a low voice to Mira, 'My apologies. I behaved badly.'

He had expected her to blush and murmur that he was forgiven, but she looked directly at him and said, 'I do not know, my lord, which is more insulting, the kiss or apologizing for it.'

He gave a reluctant laugh. 'You are wasted on Danby.'

'Indeed! I find him all that is pleasant. In fact, I think we would deal very well together. The engagement of Charles and Drusilla, which will be in the newspapers tomorrow, has brought me to my senses. I feel I have grown up. For the first time I have begun to consider

86

marriage a pleasing prospect.'

'With Mr. Danby?' The marquess all at once felt like some species of aging roué.

'He is so cheerful and pleasant, I think we could be friends. I would have my own establishment. And children!'

The marquess wondered how many more blows to the solar plexus this minx was going to deal him. Did she know anything about the *begetting* of children?

'You would like children?'

'Any woman would,' said Mira. 'I would like a son and two girls.'

'Have you told Mr. Danby of your ambitions?'

'I have only begun to speak to him,' said Mira with a giggle. 'Oh, you are about to remind me of my manners.' And she turned away to the gentleman on her other side, and the marquess, who had not been going to do any such thing, turned with some reluctance to *his* other companion.

Mira's other supper companion was a thin, nervous youth at his first ball. He was painfully shy, and Mira set to draw him out with such success that he was soon talking to her easily. The marquess began to wonder if Mira had forgotten his very existence.

But when she turned back to him, he found he could no longer be easy with her. He tried to keep his eyes away from that beautiful mouth of hers. That was the seductive thing about Mira, he thought. One kept finding little bits of beauty here and there until one could never believe that one had ever thought her plain. Drusilla, on the other hand, was beautiful for all to see, but she had a shallow character. There was nothing further to discover, nothing to excite.

Charles, sitting next to Drusilla, noticed the way the marquess studied Mira so intently and said to his fiancée, 'I do believe that Grantley is falling in love with Mira.'

'Nonsense!' said Drusilla roundly. 'He is too sophisticated and worldly a man to be attracted by a little hoyden like Mira.'

'Mira has changed,' he said thoughtfully. 'She has suddenly become more . . . womanly.'

Drusilla said huffily, 'Dear me. One would almost think you were regretting having proposed to me and would prefer Mira.'

'Don't be ridiculous.'

'Don't call me ridiculous!'

'But, my sweeting, the very idea . . .'

'All *I* know is that you suddenly seem to be watching every move that Mira makes!'

'You are jealous!'

'I! Jealous of *Mira*? Fiddlesticks. I am accounted the belle of the Season!'

She should not have said that, thought Charles gloomily. A beauty talking about her own beauty suddenly loses a good deal of it. Drusilla turned a white shoulder on him and began to talk to the man on her other side.

Charles turned his attention back to Mira. The marquess was smiling at her with a caressing look in his eyes. Mira's white gown had touches of her favorite green. Her skin was very pure and white, and that unfashionably generous mouth of hers was curved in a smile. The silent young man on her other side was darting adoring little looks at her and trying timidly to get her attention. A little down the table from her sat Mr. Danby, who kept craning his neck forward to get a look at her. Charles felt uneasy. The pride in having secured the latest London beauty for his own was waning a little. People admired Drusilla's looks. He could not imagine anyone *adoring* her.

Wrapped in his own worried thoughts, he forgot to pay attention to Drusilla or the lady on his other side. He had not really considered this thing called love seriously. That was a matter for poets and playwrights, surely. One found a pretty girl of suitable rank and fortune and settled down. Why now, as he looked across the room at Mira, did his army life call to him, the life he was on the point of rejecting? He frowned. His life, which had stretched out in front of him in an uncomplicated way, now seemed rather flat and dull. He resolved to dance with Mira. It was only right as her future brother-in-law that he should afford her a dance.

But when they all returned to the ballroom,

he discovered he could not get near Mira for the rest of the night. Drusilla found she had the humiliation of sitting out for three whole dances. The news of her engagement had spread quickly. She was no longer on the marriage market. But she felt that somehow her younger sister, by eclipsing her, was all to blame.

Lady Jansen had another dance with the marquess, but he did not offer to take her driving again. Resentment and jealousy burned fiercely in her bosom. She became convinced that the marquess, whom she had met such a short time ago, would have proposed marriage had it not been for his silly infatuation with Mira.

Mira, for once free of worries and social insecurities, danced blithely on, unaware of the emotions churning about her. When her mother told her that Mr. Danby wished permission to take her driving, she looked pleased. She still did not know why the marquess had kissed her and did not want to think of it very much, apart from deciding it had been his way of teasing her, brought about by the unconventional circumstances of that ride.

Drusilla, fretting under a new burden of jealousy of her sister, said on the road home, 'Charles is most displeased with you, Mira.'

Mira gave a little sigh. 'Charles is always displeased with me these days.'

'He said he thought your behavior this evening most unbecoming.'

'What's this?' demanded Mr. Markham sharply. 'I received many compliments about Mira. She behaved just as she ought. I must tax Charles with this.'

'Oh, do not do that!' cried Drusilla in alarm. 'He swore me to secrecy.'

'He is shortly to be my son-in-law, and he cannot go about criticizing Mira behind my back. I shall talk most severely to him about this.'

'Well, well, you see,' mumbled Drusilla, 'perhaps I was mistaken. He may have been talking about someone else.'

'You just made that up,' said Mira suddenly. 'Why?'

'I was mistaken,' shrieked Drusilla. 'Let that be an end to the matter.'

Mira gave another sigh. How complicated life had become. She thought briefly of the marquess and then put him firmly out of her mind. She had amused him, that was all, but he had given her very good advice, and for that she was grateful. She would no longer rebel. She would do just as she ought and secure a husband. She leaned back in the carriage and let rosy dreams of a home of her own, children of her own, and dogs and horses of her own float before her eyes, never stopping to wonder why there was no husband in the picture.

*　　　*　　　*

Heavily veiled, Lady Jansen set out the next day for an address in Bloomsbury. She could have summoned Diggs to her home, but she did not want any of the servants to see him. When she found concrete proof that the marquess was having an affair with Mira Markham, then when the scandal broke, there must be no way she could be implicated as the breaker of the scandal.

The hack she had hired stopped in front of a tall building. To her relief it looked trim and neat. She had feared she might find herself in a noisome slum.

Mr. Diggs, an urchin told her, resided on the top floor. She made her way up the shallow wooden stairs on the inside of the building.

As she raised her hand to knock at Diggs's door, she hesitated for a moment. It was not too late to turn back. But if Mira was not exposed and sent away, then the marquess would remain a bachelor.

She knocked loudly and then heard footsteps shuffling toward the door on the other side. The door opened, and an old man stood looking at her.

'Mr. Diggs?' she asked, peering beyond him.

'The same.'

She was disappointed. She had expected a hard sort of ferrety man, not this old man in his nightgown with white hair in elflocks. His face was paper-white and his eyes a faded blue, but at least he showed no signs of being a heavy drinker.

'I am Lady Jansen,' she said. 'I have a job for you.'

He bowed and stood aside. 'Step in, my lady. Had you sent your footman with a note, then I would have been dressed to receive you.'

'Secrecy is important.' She sailed past him into a sparsely furnished room and took a chair by the fire.

'A moment of your time,' he said. He disappeared into a far room while Lady Jansen waited impatiently, anxious now to set the wheels in motion.

At last he returned, washed and dressed with his white hair tied back with a black ribbon. He was wearing a buff suit of clothes and old-fashioned square-toed shoes.

'How may I be of assistance to you?' he asked.

She took a deep breath and told him about Mira and the marquess—what she had seen and what she suspected. He listened calmly to her, his hands on his knees, his pale eyes fixed on her face.

'Are you not going to take notes?' she demanded when she had finished.

'I may be old,' he said, 'but I have a very good memory. We must fix a price, my lady.'

He named a sum that made her blink. She looked contemptuously about the spare room.

'Oh, no,' he said, 'I am not poor and am constantly kept busy with this and that. I choose to live simply. I am not going to haggle, my lady. Those are my terms.'

'Very well,' she said.

'Half in advance,' said Mr. Diggs. 'Do not look offended. I am used to dealing with members of society who never pay their bills. Although I am sure this does not apply to you, my lady.'

'I will return with the money,' she said somewhat huffily. 'I do not carry such a sum around with me.'

'As soon as you do,' replied Mr. Diggs equably, 'then I can begin work. You must also realize that lack of success does not mean a reduction in my fees. It may be that there is nothing in this.'

'What can you mean? I saw them!'

'To put it crudely, my lady, you did not see them in bed together. The marquess was probably telling the truth when he said that Mira Markham had acted as his tiger. He seems to have been amused by the headstrong folly of a young girl, nothing more. But I assure you that if there is any truth in your allegations that they are having an affair, then I will find it.'

'How?'

'By very hard work, watching, questioning, and bribery of the servants.'

'Well ... well ... I suppose I must be

satisfied with that.' She stood up, and he rose as well. 'I shall return with your money.'

He walked to the door, bowed, and held it open for her.

When she had left, he sat down at a table in the middle of the room and began to make notes. It was his little vanity to tell clients he remembered everything. A nice little job. He had taken Lady Jansen in dislike, but then he did not often like his clients. They were motivated either by greed or jealousy.

As he expected, she returned quite shortly with the money. 'When do I get my first report?' she demanded.

'As soon as I have information for you, my lady.'

'But how will you contact me? I do not want you to come to my home or to be seen with me.'

They never did, he thought cynically. Aloud he said, 'I will send you a message by hand in a sealed letter suggesting where we should meet.'

'Very well. Do not fail me.'

'The only reason I can fail you, my lady, is if I find there is nothing in it.'

And with that she had to be content.

As soon as she had left, he pulled a slouch hat down over his eyes, took his silver-knobbed cane in his hand, and set out. He made his way on foot to the West End of London, and by dint of inquiries in the coffeehouses and taverns frequented by servants, he found the addresses of both the Marquess of Grantley and Miss Mira Markham.

The investigation had begun. He cast a fleeting thought to this Miss Mira and wondered if she deserved what was coming to her. But if she proved innocent, then she had nothing to fear.

He had no intention of fabricating evidence to please such as Lady Jansen.

CHAPTER FIVE

During the next two weeks Mr. Diggs began to think he would never receive the second half of that payment.

There was nothing to report.

The marquess was seen out driving with various ladies, including Lady Jansen. He did not take Mira driving once.

Mira Markham appeared everything that was correct. She went out several times to Hyde Park at the fashionable hour with a young Mr. Danby; she went to balls and parties. Mr. Diggs watched and listened and bribed to no avail. Everyone could tell the story about how she had pushed her sister into that fishpond, but it was repeated in a half-indulgent, half-admiring way, the servants taking their tone from their employers. The

96

weather had turned unseasonably cold, and Mr. Diggs was beginning to feel his age. Nothing was going to happen, and nothing had happened.

But in the heart of Lady Jansen, the Marquess of Grantley and Miss Mira Markham were churning emotions that did not appear on the surface.

Lady Jansen could no longer, on the face of it, blame Mira for holding the marquess's affections. The marquess did not drive with her, stand up for dances with her, or take her in for supper. So he should have been concentrating on her, Lady Jansen. But although he took her out driving a couple of times and stood up with her for dances, his manner was always polite and not very interested. She sent angry little notes to Mr. Diggs, complaining that the couple must be meeting in secret, although she was beginning to think that, after all, jealousy had made her think she had recognized Mira in a mere boy that the marquess had been talking to in Covent Garden that night.

Mira's initial happiness that she was doing just as she ought by encouraging the attentions of Mr. Danby faded fast. She was glad she was free of her longing for Charles. But she also felt her feelings for Mr. Danby should be warmer. Her heart did not beat faster when she saw him. He was pleasant, he was kind, he was good—so why did she find him so dull?

97

She could not imagine him going for midnight rides. She was more sharply aware now of the marquess's good looks than she had been before. She felt sad that he was keeping away from her. Had he been deliberately keeping away from her, then Mira would have found that a comfort, but he seemed uninterested in her, as if he saw her much as he saw the other debutantes, charming but not worth making an effort to court.

The marquess was becoming steadily more bored by the Season. It had seemed at the beginning as if it might be fun, but it had become tedious, and he was tired of empty chatter in overheated rooms. He had stayed away from Mira so that she could concentrate on young Danby. At the end of two weeks, he was asking himself why he had bothered. Mira had ceased even to notice him, or so he thought.

And so at the end of that two weeks, as he set out to a ball given by the Hays, who lived two doors away from him in Grosvenor Square, he had persuaded himself that it would be only polite to talk to her again and see how she went on. He also felt it to be his duty to warn her about her future brother-in-law. The marquess had noticed that Lord Charles always danced twice with Mira, and when he was not dancing with her or dutifully dancing with her sister, he stood around the edges of the ballroom, covertly watching Mira.

She could have had the idiot, he thought angrily, but it was just as well he had proposed to Drusilla, because he was a pompous stick. And so the ball, which was going to make Mr. Diggs's job more enjoyable, was about to take place.

Viscount and Viscountess Hay were very rich and had only one daughter, so no expense had been spared on the ball. Neil Gow and his band were to play on the balcony above the ballroom; Gunter's was to do the catering. Exotic flowers in ceramic pots of wonderful colors and glazes lined the silk-hung walls. Indian servants in turbans and exotic livery formed a guard of honor at the entrance. The ballroom floor was like a carpet under its intricate pattern of colored French chalks, soon to be dispersed by the feet of the dancers. Their daughter, Harriet, was plain but possessed of an enormous dowry, which they knew assured the girl of a certain success.

Mr. Markham was an old friend of Viscount Hay's, which was why he and his family had been invited. The Hays entertained only the cream of society. Extra special ball gowns had been ordered for Drusilla and Mira. Drusilla, who was becoming increasingly bad-tempered and jealous, found it hard to contain her temper when she saw Mira's ball gown. It consisted of a white silk underdress with an overdress of silver net embroidered with green sequins in a leaf pattern. Her headdress was a coronet of gold wire and green silk leaves. Mira had called on the dressmaker in person to sketch out what she wanted. Drusilla had left the choice, as usual, to her mother and had a pretty gown of white muslin with bands of white satin. She looked exquisite, but jealousy made her believe that Mira looked the more dramatic of the two. She said nothing, having learned to curb her tongue in front of her father, but she kept darting angry little glances at Mira as they set out.

Charles was in the carriage with them. Mr. Markham asked idly, 'Sold out yet, Charles?' and to Drusilla's surprise she heard her fiancé say, 'Not yet.'

'Why not?' she demanded acidly. 'I do not want to be married to a soldier.'

'You must give me time, my dear,' said Charles.

'Why?' demanded Drusilla. 'Why do you need time? One letter and a draft from your bank are enough, surely?'

'Drusilla,' admonished Mr. Markham.

'You do not seem to realize,' said Charles with an edge to his voice, 'that I love my regiment.'

'More than you love me?'

'That is not fair. I said I would sell out.'

'It must be a sad wrench to leave all one's comrades,' said Mira sympathetically.

Drusilla glared at her. 'Who asked you?'

'That was very rude, dear,' said Mrs.

100

Markham.

Drusilla burst into overwrought tears, and it was only Mira's voice saying in her ear, 'We are nearly there, and you will look like a guy with your eyes all red' that made her force herself to dry her tears and compose herself.

As they waited in the hall of the Hays' mansion for the ladies, Mr. Markham said to Charles, 'You must forgive Drusilla. She is good at heart. I blame myself and my wife for spoiling her.'

Charles only nodded. He was thinking sourly that if they had ignored Drusilla during her upbringing in the way they had ignored Mira, then Drusilla might have turned out as charming in soul as she was in appearance.

Mira and Drusilla emerged. Charles, who had only seen Mira cloaked before they left the Markhams' home, stood for a moment looking at her and then walked forward in a dazed way. Mr. Markham thought dismally that if Drusilla had not quickly stepped forward to take his arm, then Charles would have forgotten about all of them except Mira and would have held out his arm to her.

The marquess watched them enter. He would favor Mira with a dance and take her in to supper, he thought, just to see how she went on. It was only polite. But he left it too late. He had not taken Mira's ever-increasing popularity into account. She did not have a single dance free. 'Who have you honored with the supper dance?' he asked.

'Mr. Danby.'

The marquess bowed and left. Mira watched him go before turning to her next partner and tried to ignore the odd little tug at her heart. The marquess did not feel like dancing. He was aware of Lady Jansen looking hopefully toward him. He went into the card room and joined a group of men watching the play. To his surprise one of the players at a game of hazard dice was young Danby.

He turned to Lord Minster, a tall peer standing next to him, and nodded in Mr. Danby's direction. 'That one never struck me as a gambler.'

'The silly pup plays deep,' said Lord Minster. 'He drinks too much and can't keep a cool head.'

The marquess began to worry. He had encouraged Mira to cast her lot with someone who showed all the hallmarks of a budding hardened gambler. He moved toward the table, and when one of the men got up and said ruefully that he had lost enough, the marquess took his place. He began to win almost immediately and bet more and more until only he and Mr. Danby were left against each other.

When Mr. Danby finally found he had lost over five thousand pounds to the marquess, it seemed to sober him. 'I will need to g-give you m-my note of hand,' he stammered. And then almost half to himself, he said wretchedly, 'I do not know what my parents will say.'

The marquess quickly looked around. The watchers, now that the play was over, had gone to observe a game of piquet at another table.

'Danby, you can recoup your losses,' he said.

'How, my lord?'

'I will buy your supper dance.'

'For how much?'

'For the sum you owe me.'

Relief and mortification struggled oddly in Mr. Danby's ingenuous face. 'Why do you want to dance with Miss Mira so much?' he demanded.

'I am a friend of the family's,' said the marquess with seeming indifference. 'Furthermore I have never had the reputation of fleecing young men and do not wish to start now. What is it to be?'

'You will not tell anyone? I would feel such a fool.'

'You should feel even more of a fool for losing such a sum to me. But you have my word on it.'

Neither noticed a footman hovering behind them. The footman was well aware that there was an ex-Runner willing to pay for any information about this marquess. The fact that the Marquess of Grantley was willing to pay well over five thousand pounds for a dance with Miss Mira Markham should be worth a good reward.

'Very well,' said Mr. Danby. 'But what will you tell her?'

'I shall tell her that you are feeling unwell and have begged me to take your place. That is all.'

And so Mira looked up in surprise when she was approached by the marquess later that evening, who told her solemnly that Mr. Danby was feeling poorly and had begged him to take his place.

Lady Jansen watched bitterly as the marquess led Mira onto the floor. She hoped Diggs was doing his job. She even began to worry that the guilty couple had found out about him and had bribed him to give her innocent reports.

When the marquess took Mira into the supper room, he carefully maneuvered her toward the end of one of the tables so that she would have no companion on her side, and on his other side there was deaf old Lady Antrim, who never talked to anyone anyway.

'How do you go on?' he began.

'Tolerably well,' said Mira. 'I am behaving like an angel.'

'You must be enjoying your popularity.'

'I am only human. Of course, my lord.'

'I fear I misled you about young Danby. I thought he would prove to be all that was suitable.'

'And he is not?'

'I fear he is already showing signs of being a

hardened gambler who cannot hold his drink.'

She laughed. 'Now that I find hard to believe!'

'I do not expect you to believe me. Do not rush into marriage with him. Do not encourage him anymore until you have studied him a little further.'

Those green eyes flashed with mockery. 'Yes, Father.'

'Jade! Admit you are not shocked or startled or hurt by my news. You feel nothing for Mr. Danby.'

She looked at him cynically. 'Am I meant to? I did not think love entered into a Society marriage.'

'It sometimes does. Lord Charles and your sister, I suppose, are typical.'

'Of a love match?'

'Of a loveless arrangement.'

'I think you are mistaken. Charles is willing to sell out, and all for love of Drusilla.'

'Have some more wine. I think you will find Lord Charles became engaged in haste and is now repenting his decision at leisure.' He wondered now whether to warn Mira that Lord Charles was becoming infatuated with her. He decided against it. Those wonderful eyes of hers might light up with gladness.

The weather after the miserable preceding two weeks had turned fine and warm. The long windows at the end of the supper room were open, and balmy air blew in, sending the candle flames streaming.

'Shall I get a footman to close those windows?' asked the marquess.

Mira shook her head. 'I love fresh air, any fresh air, even London air. I have been feeling cribbed, cabined, and confined of late.'

'Have you forgiven me for that kiss?'

She blushed and pleated a fold of the tablecloth between nervous fingers. 'I suppose so. But it was wicked of you to make fun of me.'

'I was not making fun of you. I forgot myself. But I enjoyed riding with you.'

Her eyes shone. 'I wanted to ride again, even in the Row, but Mama said it was not suitable and I must put my wild ways behind me. But I find it hard to let so much of my old self go. I feel if I could have just one more day of freedom, I could face the idea of settling down with equanimity.'

The warm air flowed about them. The marquess felt a tingling of excitement. 'Are you bored with all this?' he asked, and waved a hand, encompassing London's finest and Gunter's catering.

'Oh, yes.'

'Perhaps we could arrange something.'

'Such as?'

He thought quickly. He knew that what he was about to suggest was, in the words of Lady Caroline Lamb about Lord Byron, mad, bad, and dangerous. But he said it nonetheless.

'Has your family been invited to go tomorrow on the Earl of Hardforth's barge outing?'

'Yes, we are to join the barge quite early and sail up the Thames to Hampton Court. It will take all day.'

'You could plead a headache and join me. Put on those riding clothes I gave you, and we could ride out of London and be free.'

Her heart beat hard. 'You will not do anything like . . . like . . .?'

'Kiss you? No, my sweeting. I will lead that Arab you liked so much to Hyde Park toll and meet you there. Now what time?'

'Ten,' said Mira. 'At ten in the morning. They are not due to return until late.'

'Make sure the servants do not see you leave!'

'Be assured. I will tell them not to disturb me at all. I will lock the door of my room behind me.'

'Will you leave by the back door?'

'No. As soon as they have all left, our servants will go to their own hall for tea. There will be no one about. I can slip out by the front door.'

He looked at her doubtfully. 'I fear I am leading you astray.'

'Just one day of freedom will not matter. No one will find out, and after it I will be an even more correct young lady than before. Tell me, if Mr. Danby is such a bad prospect, whom do you recommend?'

107

His eyes roamed about the room. 'There is Mr. Jessop, who is young, wealthy, and has already had two dances with you.'

'I did not notice him particularly. Which is he?'

'The tall young man four seats away from your sister, with thick brown hair and a plum-colored silk coat.'

'Ah, yes, he pressed my hand rather hard in the promenade. I fear he is too forward.'

'The devil he did!'

'Who else?'

'There is that young baronet, Sir Giles Parry. He is quiet and good.'

'And dull.'

'You have become hard to please, Mira Markham.'

'Perhaps I shall be a spinster after all. That would not please my father.'

'From what you have told me, your whole young life has been devoted to trying to please your father.'

'I think he has become fond of me,' she said wistfully. 'I hope so.'

The marquess stopped himself with a conscious effort from saying that he thought Mr. Markham a most unnatural parent.

'Be very careful you are not seen,' he warned.

After supper Mira's next dance was with Charles. It was a waltz. She wondered as she danced with him why it was that she should no longer feel anything for him. Perhaps it was because he had chosen the role of cross elderly brother. She was dreamily looking forward to her day of escape on the following day and hoping the ball would not go on very long so that she could get a few hours' sleep when Charles interrupted her thoughts by saying, 'You are looking very beautiful tonight, Mira.'

She looked up at him, her eyes glowing with simple pleasure at the compliment. 'Why, thank you, Charles!'

'If I had known . . . but no matter. You seem to be close to Grantley.'

'He is a friend, as you once were, Charles.'

'You hurt me, Mira. I am still your friend.'

Mira laughed. 'Pooh, you think I am a silly little girl.'

His hand holding hers tightened. 'You have become a woman, Mira, an intriguing and attractive woman.'

'Thank you,' she said, looking every bit as uncomfortable as she felt. 'You are holding my hand too tightly, Charles.'

'I beg your pardon,' he said miserably.

Mira wondered what had come over him. Then she thought he had probably drunk too much. Gentlemen behaved strangely in their cups.

But she was glad when the dance was over.

The marquess was dancing with Lady Jansen, a fact that made Mira cross. Lady Jansen had spread gossip. The marquess should ignore her, not dance with her as if she were the only woman in the room!

But she comforted herself with the thought of that outing tomorrow and then realized that if she was to pretend to be ill and have a headache, she should start pretending right away.

Mrs. Markham was sympathetic. She wanted to leave the ball herself, also anxious to get some sleep before such an indecently early start in the morning. Drusilla was glad to leave as well. She was disappointed in Charles. She expected adoration from him—uncritical adoration at all times.

Mira was glad to pretend she was feeling unwell because it saved making conversation on the road home. But when Mrs. Markham came to see her as she lay in bed and showed rare signs of motherly concern, Mira felt a pang of guilt but assured her mother if she could forgo the barge trip and have a quiet day in bed, then she would come about.

Mrs. Markham agreed, not only because she believed Mira to be ill but because she was increasingly worried about Lord Charles's manner toward Drusilla and his evident growing interest in Mira. A romantic day on the river was just what Charles and Drusilla needed.

As soon as her mother had left, Mira got out of bed and searched in a trunk at the bottom of the press, where she had hidden the riding clothes. She would lock the door and take the key when she left, just to be safe.

She slept and woke and slept and woke, listening all the time to the harsh voice of the watchman marking off the hours.

Then she heard the house come awake and Drusilla's voice raised in complaint as she berated the maid. Mrs. Markham came in, dressed for the expedition. Mira pretended to be asleep and lay with her eyes closed until her mother had left. Then she got out of bed, washed, dressed in the riding clothes, and sat down in front of the mirror on the toilet table to tie her cravat. It was rather tired-looking, not having been laundered or starched since the last time she had worn it.

*   *   *

Mr. Diggs was at his post in St. James's Square early the following morning. He had been excited by the footman's news that the marquess was prepared to let a gambling debt of five thousand pounds go in order to secure a dance with Miss Mira. He debated whether to watch the marquess's house and then decided on the Markhams'. He knew of the barge expedition and planned to follow the family party on horseback to London Bridge and then ride to Hampton Court and study them there.

He saw Lord Charles arriving, the carriage being brought round, and then the Markhams and Lord Charles setting out. His eyes sharpened. No Mira. As they drove off, he wondered whether to follow them but decided to wait. Perhaps Mira was going to use this opportunity to slip off and see her lover.

He was just wondering whether he ought to go and try to question one of the servants when the front door opened and a slim youth scampered down the stairs. It was only when the 'youth' reached the corner of the square and turned and looked cautiously back that he saw those green eyes. He had nearly missed her. Lady Jansen said she had been dressed as a boy in Covent Garden.

He swung up into the saddle and began to follow her.

At Hyde Park Corner he saw with a feeling of triumph the tall figure of the Marquess of Grantley standing beside the toll holding two horses. He eyed those horses. They were magnificent, but the marquess surely would not drive them hard along the gravel surface of the Great West Road, if that was the way he meant to go.

He saw the way the couple greeted each other like conspirators, and then Mira sprang nimbly up on the back of the Arab.

Mr. Diggs set off in pursuit, glad that they were taking an easy pace. But after Knightsbridge, the marquess shouted something, and they set off across the fields. Diggs spurred his mount, but there was no way

112

he could catch up with them. He wondered what to do. He needed corroborative evidence. His own word would not be enough. They could both deny the whole thing.

But Mira could not be absent a whole day without the servants knowing. Perhaps she had pleaded sickness and locked the door of her bedchamber. So if he returned to St. James's Square claiming to have a message for her that she must receive from him personally, the game would be up.

But would it?

All Mira had to do would be to admit that, yes, she had been lying but that she wanted to be on her own for a day.

Perhaps if they stopped somewhere, at some inn, he could catch up with them. He set off again in the direction they had taken.

*   *   *

The marquess and Mira were sitting on a grassy bank above a wind of the River Thames. 'I did enjoy that,' said Mira, stretching her arms above her head to the blue sky. 'I must find a husband who will let me ride *ventre à terre.*'

He laughed. 'I will tell your future. You will become a respectable matron in no time at all with children in the nursery. You will become plump and placid and go on calls to the neighboring gentry, and you will be very strict with your daughters, always suspecting them of getting into the same scrapes you got into yourself.'

'Not I. I would like freedom.'

'I do not think you are going to get it, such is the lot of women,' said the marquess. 'Or you will stay a spinster and be expected to behave until your parents die. Then the money will go to Drusilla's son, and you will have a small competence. You will travel abroad with your sketchbook, just another English spinster with a sketchbook, lonely and awkward and unable to go for wild rides, for you will have stiffened up with genteel activity.'

'And what if I marry?'

'Your husband may admire your wildness before marriage, but after marriage he will expect you to be correct in all things.'

'Would you?'

'Ah, yes, I am as bad as the rest. I would expect my wife to be a gracious hostess and run my household for me.'

'Sad! Let us not talk of the future. There is only today. What are we going to do?'

'We are shortly going to find a comfortable inn on the river and eat and drink something, and then we shall see.'

She lay back and stared up at the sky. Her coat fell open, and he turned his eyes away quickly from the young swell of her breasts and looked out across the river. 'Your family will be well on their way,' he said.

'Yes,' she said idly.

'Do you often think of Lord Charles, or has that dream gone?'

'It went, just like that. He was so very stuffy, lecturing me on my behavior. I realized we had both changed. I amused him as a child and when he, too, was younger. I thought of him romantically for only a little. He will be happy with Drusilla.'

Not while he is busy falling in love with you, thought the marquess, but remained silent. He wondered how Lord Charles was coping with the absence of Mira.

*   *   *

Charles was leaning gloomily against the side of the barge, watching the greenish water of the upper reaches of the Thames slip by. He thought that Mr. and Mrs. Markham had been cruel to leave their younger daughter, who was not feeling well, alone in a houseful of servants with no one really to care for her. He had demanded angrily why the physician had not been sent for and was not reassured by Mrs. Markham's placid reply that young girls were subject to megrims occasionally and should be left in peace and quiet to recover.

The more he thought about Mira, the more he longed to leap from the barge, make his way back to London, and find out how she was. No wonder she had behaved so badly, pushing

115

Drusilla into that fishpond. He often felt like pushing her himself. What was beauty if the character that went with it was shallow and vain? And yet he had been stunned by her beauty and willing to sacrifice his army career to possess it. Although society's laws were very strict and all young ladies were supposed to be chaperoned at all times, a certain leeway was given to engaged couples and a blind eye turned to the stolen kiss. And so he had had a few moments alone with Drusilla. Eager to reanimate his brief love for her, he had taken her in his arms and pressed his lips to hers. She had stood there, passive and docile in his arms and totally unresponsive, and the moment he had released her, she had said severely, 'There is time enough for that sort of thing when we are married. Have you written to your regiment yet?'

Behind him on the black-and-gold barge a band was playing. He should be the happiest man on earth. But here he was, wondering and wondering if he could find some way to make Drusilla break the engagement. The trouble was that despite her beauty no other man seemed to be pining for her. Certainly, were she free, she would soon find suitors, but she was not the sort to inspire passion, to inspire some man to court her while she was engaged to another.

The Marquess of Grantley seemed intrigued with Mira. Charles frowned suddenly. He had felt very uneasy about the gossip that Mira had dressed in boy's clothes and acted as the marquess's tiger. He had not told anyone of her visit to his lodgings. But surely it followed that dressing up and acting as a tiger was just the sort of thing Mira would have done. He suddenly wanted to talk to her about it, that minute.

She would be alone for the rest of the day. Perhaps if *he* was to complain of illness, he could hire a carriage and horses at Hampton Court and drive back to London to see how she went on. He persuaded himself that his motives were to protect her and to find out if she had really gone out with the marquess on that race.

Drusilla and her parents joined him. 'You are very quiet, Charles,' complained Drusilla.

'I am feeling very ill,' he said, and knew as he said it that he had decided to escape.

CHAPTER SIX

While Charles was planning his escape back to London, Mira and the marquess had found a pleasant little inn by the river. They were seated at a table in the garden, eating cold meat pie washed down with porter.

'Would it not be wonderful to live like this the whole time?' said Mira.

117

'Endless holiday? You would soon become bored, my sweeting.'

'I was thinking more of freedom from society's restrictions. It does not affect you, my lord, for you are a man.'

'You noticed?' His eyes mocked her, and she said severely, 'You know exactly what I mean. On the face of it the ballroom is a pleasant and romantic place, but when I am tired, I see it for what it is—a cattle market, with us, the debutantes, the placid cows, waiting for a buyer. We really have no say in our futures. We dare not choose a husband—or rather be chosen—if our parents do not consider him up to the mark. You can leave it all and go riding or forget about the whole thing and return to your estates.'

'Fretting about your lot is going to spoil the day,' said the marquess. 'You eat so much! Do you plan to lie down on the grass afterward and sleep?'

She laughed. 'Not I.' Her eyes fell on a rowing boat tied to a stump beside the river. 'I would like to take that boat out.'

'Can you row or even swim?'

'Neither, but you could teach me to row.'

He looked doubtfully at the rapidly moving water. 'The current is quite swift here, and the boat looks leaky.'

'Oh, do let us try!'

'You are an impetuous child, Mira. Finish your food and we will see.'

During the following days the marquess was to think ruefully that he must have been possessed by temporary madness. Had he not agreed to Mira's request, then all might have been well.

But as it was, he gave in and asked the landlord if they might hire his boat, and soon Mira was being given her first instruction in rowing. At first it all seemed easy, for they were going with the current, but when the marquess suggested they turn about and head back, Mira found she could not cope with the strength of the river.

'We will need to change places,' said the marquess. Mira clumsily shipped the oars and got to her feet.

'Careful,' he warned. 'Perhaps you should crawl forward.'

A barge had passed them on the river, and as Mira got to her feet, the swell from it hit the rowing boat, which lurched and catapulted her into the water. 'Help!' spluttered Mira.

He dived overboard and swam to her. 'Don't struggle,' he shouted. 'Put your arms around my neck.' Gasping and terrified, she retained enough presence of mind to do as she was told, and he swam with her to the shore, dragging her up the bank as soon as he had found a footing.

'Stay there,' ordered the marquess. 'Let us hope that wretched boat has stopped somewhere.'

Dripping wet, Mira sat down on the bank and waited. After what seemed an age the marquess came round the bend of the river, rowing strongly. He pulled in to the shore and ordered her to get in. 'Fortunately the boat was caught under the overhanging branches of a willow,' he said. 'Now let us get back to that inn and get our clothes dried. You have lost your hat. Let us hope that landlord is blind!'

At the inn Mira stood behind the marquess while he explained the accident and requested a bedchamber where they could wait until their clothes had been dried.

The landlord rushed to accommodate them, for he had heard Mira call the marquess 'my lord'. It was not often that members of the Quality arrived at his out-of-the-way inn.

Rough towels were supplied, and Mira went behind the shelter of the bed hangings to take off her wet clothes and towel herself dry. She emerged, wrapped in a blanket, to find the marquess sitting in an armchair, also wrapped in a blanket. When the landlord reappeared, the marquess handed him their wet clothes.

'I'll get the girl to hang these in the garden, my lord,' said the landlord. 'There's a stiff breeze, and what with the hot sunshine, they'll be dry in no time at all.'

'And let's hope they don't shrink,' said the marquess after he had left. Mira sat on the floor, huddled in the blanket. He was sharply aware that she was naked under it. He got to his feet, went to a table in the corner, and picked up a pack of cards.

'I shall play you for vast sums of money,' he said lightly. 'That way we can pass the time until our clothes are dry.'

*   *   *

A weary Mr. Diggs arrived at the inn. He was so tired and thirsty, he no longer cared where Mira and the marquess had got to. He ordered a pint of shrub after seeing to his horse, took his drink out to the sunny garden, and sat down with a sigh of relief. He would soon be too old for work like this, he thought.

He glanced idly around. At the side of the inn, a clothesline was stretched between two trees, and as he watched, a little maid came out and began to hang up clothes. Then he slowly put down his tankard and sat up straight as he watched those clothes as they were pinned out on the line, one by one.

He rose and walked around to the back of the inn. He had been so tired, he had stabled his horse without paying any attention to the other mounts. This time he immediately recognized the Arab Mira had been riding.

Mr. Diggs went into the cool darkness of the inn and hailed the landlord.

'I have reason to believe that there is a scandal here in your inn to be uncovered,

121

landlord,' he said, 'and if you help me, there is gold in it for you.'

The landlord listened to the tale of Mira and the marquess with his eyes popping. 'Sounds like a right fairy tale to me, sir,' he said, scratching his head. 'I mean, young ladies don't ride around like boys. I don't want no trouble. What if you're telling lies?'

'Where are they now?' demanded Mr. Diggs, mentally damning all yokels.

'There in my best bedchamber, wrapped in blankets and waiting for their clothes to dry.'

'So? So did you not notice she's got hair like a woman?'

'Got it in a pigtail, but a lot of men still wear their hair that way.'

'Look, fellow, there is money in this for you. I need a written statement from you, and I will pay you five gold guineas for it. Go abovestairs and ask them if they would like a fire if you have not already lit one.'

The landlord hesitated, but five guineas seemed like a fortune to him. He went upstairs while Mr. Diggs waited impatiently.

When the landlord entered the room, Mira and the marquess were sitting on the floor, playing cards. But the room was in half darkness, for the curtains were closed.

'What is it?' demanded the marquess sharply.

'I was wondering whether you would like me to light the fire, my lord?'

122

'No, go away, and don't come back until our clothes are dried.'

'Dark in here,' commented the landlord. Before the marquess could protest, he had crossed the floor and jerked open the curtains. Sunlight flooded the room. The landlord turned and stared down at Mira, who bent her head quickly over her cards.

'Get out of here!' shouted the marquess. The landlord beat a hasty retreat.

He went downstairs and joined Mr. Diggs in the tap. 'You've the right of it,' he said heavily. 'I got a good look at her. Such goings-on in a respectable inn!'

'Look, fellow,' said Mr. Diggs, 'what is your name?'

'Giles Brand.'

'Well, Mr. Brand, if you want to earn your money, fetch quill, ink, and paper, and I will tell you what to write.'

*   *   *

'Damn!' said the marquess, throwing down his cards. 'I want to get out of here. I don't trust that fellow. I'll swear he opened those curtains to get a better look at you. Why on earth did I agree to this expedition?'

'You suggested it,' said Mira in a small voice.

'Let us hope we escape with our reputations intact. At least he does not know who we are.'

123

Mira brightened. 'Of course he doesn't. How much money have you won from me?'

'Thousands and thousands. It is as well it is pretend money. You would never make a gambler.'

Mira stood up and went to the window, the large blanket trailing behind her. 'How long now before our clothes dry, do you think?'

'I think we should get them back and put them on, whatever their condition, and get out of here. I do not like that landlord's behavior.'

The marquess went to the door, opened it, and shouted, 'Bring up our clothes. Never mind if they are still damp.'

When the landlord came up with the clothes, the marquess scrutinized him, but Mr. Brand had been warned by Mr. Diggs not to evince any more curiosity in the pair in case they found some way to cover up the scandal—by which Mr. Diggs really meant he did not want this wealthy marquess bribing the landlord to silence and hoped that the landlord did not realize that he stood to gain more money from the marquess than he could ever get from him. The marquess was reassured. There were no suspicious looks here.

He and Mira dressed hurriedly. Their clothes were damp and uncomfortable.

They left together and walked down to the tap. The marquess paid the landlord for their food, the room, and the hire of the boat. Mira waited for him in the open doorway. She was aware of being observed and turned her eyes to a shadowy corner of the tap. An elderly man sat there. He quickly looked down at the table. Mira frowned. There was something vaguely familiar about him. She felt she had seen him, and only recently at that.

The marquess joined her, and they went out together into the sunshine.

'Our adventures are over,' said the marquess. 'Time for you to return home and become a respectable young miss again.'

Mira looked about the sunny inn yard. 'I will never forget this day,' she said in a wistful voice.

'I pray that you can reach your room unobserved,' he said as they rode off together.

'I do not expect any trouble. The servants are probably enjoying a day off,' said Mira. 'No one will see me arrive.'

*   *   *

Lord Charles faced the Markhams' butler. 'I demand to see Miss Mira,' he said. 'She may be much more ill than her parents realized.'

'But, my lord, her door is locked.'

'You have spare keys surely?'

'Yes, my lord, but—'

'I insist.'

The butler summoned a footman and asked him to bring the key to Miss Mira's bedchamber. Charles was aware that the butler was exuding an air of disapproval and knew the man was wondering why Lord Charles was not still with the Markham family party.

The footman returned with the key, and the butler led the way upstairs.

He stopped outside Mira's bedchamber and rapped loudly on the door. Then he and Charles stood side by side listening to the silence.

'Open the door!' demanded Charles impatiently.

The butler unlocked the door and held it open. Charles strode into the room. The bed curtains were closed, and he drew them back. At first it seemed as if Mira was lying asleep. He crossed to the window and threw back the shutters. Sunlight streamed into the room. He returned to the bed and with one angry movement whipped back the covers to reveal a bolster attached to a cushion with a nightcap on it to serve as a head.

'There is your Miss Mira,' he said angrily. 'Where is she?'

The butler looked bewildered. 'I am sure I do not know, my lord.'

'I will wait for her,' said Charles, sitting down in a chair and crossing his arms.

*   *   *

Mira said a polite good-bye to the marquess at Hyde Park toll and made her way through the busy streets, wishing she still had her hat.

The riding clothes had shrunk slightly. She was looking forward to getting out of them. She went round the back of the house in St. James's Square and let herself in quietly by the garden door. She made her way swiftly up the back stairs, praying she would not meet one of the servants. She gained the security of her room, walked in, and slammed the door behind her. She leaned her back against the panels with a sigh of relief. One split second before she saw Charles, she realized the door of her bedchamber should still have been locked.

And then she did see Charles. His face was stern, and he looked her up and down, from the top of her tousled head down to her crumpled and shrunken riding clothes.

'What is the meaning of this?' he demanded.

Mira quickly got over the first shock of seeing him.

She opened the door again and swung back to him. 'What is the meaning of *this*, Charles, may I ask? What are you doing in my bedchamber?'

'I was worried about you and came to see how you were. I discovered your deception, Mira. Where have you been and in such clothes? Have you no shame?'

'You are not yet a member of this family, nor have you any right to give me a jaw-me-dead, Charles. If you must know, I wanted some freedom, some time to myself. Hardly a heinous crime.'

'You have been with him!'

'What are you talking about?' demanded Mira coolly, although her heart was racing.

'Grantley. You have been with Grantley.'

'What fustian you talk. Get out of here, Charles, until I change my clothes.'

'I shall wait belowstairs for the return of your parents.' He walked up to her. Those green eyes, which had only lately begun to fascinate him, stared defiantly up at him. He caught her to him. 'Oh, Mira,' he said huskily, 'we could deal together better than this.'

She tore herself free of his grasp and said, 'By all means wait for my parents, Charles. They will be interested to learn of your shameful behavior, perhaps more interested than they will be in mine.'

He turned red with mortification. 'I forgot myself,' he said wretchedly. 'Forgive me. Look, I will say nothing to your parents if you forget my lapse.'

'Then you must explain to the servants that mine was a simple prank and that you do not wish my parents worried, Charles.'

'I will do that. Mira, I must explain—'

She held up one small hand. 'Do not, Charles. For I fear you are about to say something unforgivable. Please go!'

*   *   *

128

Charles had given the butler a generous sum and explained matters, saying he had called to see how Miss Mira went on. There was no need to upset her parents by telling them of her childish prank. But he had forgotten to warn the butler not to mention his visit. So when Mr. and Mrs. Markham and Drusilla returned and Mrs. Markham asked, 'Did we have any callers?' the butler replied, 'Only Lord Charles, madam.'

'What?' demanded Drusilla angrily. 'He left our party because he said he was ill. What on earth was he doing calling here?'

'Lord Charles called to inquire after the health of Miss Mira.'

'That will be all,' said Mr. Markham sharply. 'If Miss Mira is recovered, tell her to join us in the drawing room.'

Mira, washed and changed and wearing a white muslin gown, entered the drawing room. Her eyes flew to Drusilla's angry face.

'Sit down, Mira,' said her father sternly.

Mira did as she was bid and tried to look puzzled and innocent.

'We are upset to learn that Charles, who said he had to leave our party at Hampton Court because he was feeling poorly, called here to find out about your health.'

Mira experienced a feeling of relief. 'Yes,' she said calmly. 'Charles takes his duties as my future brother-in-law very seriously. It was most kind of him considering that he felt peaky himself.' She turned to Drusilla. 'He is so stuffy and correct, Drusilla.'

'Well, I suppose that was kind of him,' said Mr. Markham suspiciously. 'How do you go on?'

'Much better, Papa. I thank you. How was your day?'

Mrs. Markham began to describe the beauties of Hampton Court, and Mira listened with well-feigned interest, aware the whole time that her father's suspicions had not quite been allayed. She was beginning to fret about her own behavior. She had shared a bedchamber with the Marquess of Grantley. Dear heavens, if that was ever to come out! But no one knew. All she had to do was behave correctly. But Charles was an unexpected complication. She would tell the marquess about it, and he would advise her. How odd that she should have considered herself nigh dying of love for Charles such a short time ago, and now that he seemed attracted to her, she considered it shocking and tiresome.

*　　　*　　　*

Lady Jansen met Mr. Diggs in St. James's Park the following day, Usually it was she who summoned him, but the fact that this time it was he who had sent her a note arranging the meeting was hopeful. Heavily veiled, she sat in her carriage and waited impatiently until she saw his elderly figure walking across the grass toward Birdcage Walk.

She let down the glass and signaled to him. He climbed in and sat beside her. 'Success at last,' said Mr. Diggs. She listened while he told of Mira's escapade, her face becoming a mask of fury and jealousy as he went on to tell of their sharing a bedchamber at the inn. 'And you have the statement from this landlord?' she demanded.

'Yes, my lady.'

'Let me have it!'

'When, and only when, you have paid the second half of your fee, and if you are not to be implicated in the breaking of this scandal, how do you plan to go about it?'

'I shall send the landlord's statement about this slut to her parents—anonymously.'

Very well. When do you wish to give me the money?'

Lady Jansen threw caution to the wind. 'Come back with me now,' she said. 'I must have that letter.'

Mrs. Anderson, the faded companion, looked up from a basket of mending as Lady Jansen entered with Mr. Diggs at her heels. 'Leave us,' ordered Lady Jansen curtly.

Mrs. Anderson meekly gathered up her sewing and left the room, but once outside she set down the basket at her feet and pressed her ear to the panels of the door.

'There is a draft on my bank, Mr. Diggs,' she heard Lady Jansen say. 'You have done your work well. Why did you leave the Runners?'

'I did not leave, my lady. I retired,' came Mr. Diggs's voice. 'May I say one thing about this matter? Although the fact is that Mira Markham shared a bedchamber at the Green Tree near Richmond with the Marquess of Grantley, I am persuaded it was because they both fell into the river and had to wait somewhere until their clothes were dry. I consider Miss Mira an innocent.'

And her employer's voice, harsh with fury, reached Mrs. Anderson's listening ears. 'I do not care what they did or did not do.' There was a rustle of paper. 'There is enough here to ruin the girl and send her out of London. Take your money and go, and forget you ever saw me. This letter from the landlord of that inn will finish her.'

Mrs. Anderson scuttled away from the door. She had conceived a great admiration for this wild girl, Mira, who could flout the conventions in a way that the timid Mrs. Anderson would never dream of doing. Perhaps she could be as courageous as Mira and do something to spike Lady Jansen's guns. She waited until Mr. Diggs had left and then went back to the drawing room.

'I am out of green silk, my lady,' she said in her usual humble way. 'I do not want to send one of the maids because they can never match

132

colors very well. May I have your permission to go out?'

'Yes, yes,' said Lady Jansen. She was sitting at her writing desk.

Mrs. Anderson went upstairs, put on her bonnet and cloak, and set out for Grosvenor Square. In the small world of London society, everyone knew where everyone else lived.

The marquess was dressing to go out. His butler entered and said there was a lady waiting below to see him. The marquess's thoughts flew to Mira. 'A young lady?'

'No, my lord, not young, but a lady. She would not give her name.'

'Probably collecting for some charity. I shall give her a few moments. Put her in the Blue Saloon, and tell her I will be with her presently.'

He took his time about completing his toilet and then went downstairs, entered the Blue Saloon, and looked curiously at the timid and flustered lady who rose to curtsy to him.

'My lord,' said Mrs. Anderson. 'You are in great danger.'

His first thought was that his usually correct butler had let a madwoman into his house. But when he heard her story, his face darkened, and he took mental notes. Diggs, retired Runner, must be squared, as must that landlord. Damn. Mira must be warned to deny everything until he killed the gossip.

He thanked Mrs. Anderson warmly and

then went back upstairs and changed swiftly into his riding clothes. He went straight to the Markhams, who were surprised that the marquess should have chosen to make a call in his riding dress. He fretted while he made social chitchat and then, turning to Mira, said he would like to see her drawings. Mira, who knew herself to be an incompetent artist, looked at him in surprise but went to collect her portfolio. As she bent over it, he dropped a note between the sketches and said, 'Read that,' and then, as if recollecting a pressing appointment, he abruptly took his leave.

Mira left the room immediately afterward, saying she was going to put her portfolio away and ignoring Drusilla's jeering remark that her bad drawing had sent the marquess flying on his way.

She scanned the note. 'Burn this when you have read it,' the marquess had written. 'Some ill-wisher has discovered evidence of our day together, which I am out to destroy. Deny everything.'

Her hands trembled as she lit a candle, burned his note, and crushed the ashes to powder. What could have happened? Someone must have seen them! And they had shared a bedchamber.

She went about for the next hour feeling the awful storm was about to break. And it broke at four in the afternoon, which was when Mr. Markham received a sealed packet. He opened it and read the statement of the landlord of the Green Tree, his face darkening with amazement and shock.

In the garden Mira had buried those riding clothes the marquess had given her. Summoning all her courage, she faced her wrathful father and denied the lot, hoping against hope that Charles would not arrive and be prompted by jealousy into saying he had found her dressed as a boy.

Mr. Markham sent several messages to the marquess's town house, but each time his servant returned to say the marquess was not at home.

Drusilla said she knew Mira was lying. Drusilla was praying Mira was lying. If this scandal was true, then Mira would be sent away and Charles would return to his senses. Drusilla had been becoming increasingly alarmed over the way Charles kept looking at Mira. But Mira remained obdurate. She had been ill, and she could not understand why she was not being believed by her own family. But her heart sank when Mr. Markham said that enough was enough and that he would drive to that inn and take Mira with him.

As it was, it was the whole Markham family who set out, Mrs. Markham terrified of such a scandal about one of her daughters and Drusilla determined to see the ruin of Mira.

Mira blindly kept on doing what the marquess had told her to do. But as the

Markham carriage began to lurch along the country road leading to the inn, she felt sure all would be discovered. If this landlord had gone to the lengths to make a statement of her behavior, then he was not going to back down.

She felt a lump in her throat as the inn heaved into view. How happy she had been only the day before!

They entered the tap, Mr. Markham pushing Mira before him. There were a few locals in the corner. Mr. Markham approached the landlord. 'Are you Giles Brand?'

The landlord bowed. 'The same.'

'Is this yours?' Mr. Markham slammed the statement down in front of him on a scarred table.

The landlord looked down at it with well-feigned amazement. 'Can't be mine, Your Honor.'

'Why not?'

'Reckon as how I can't write naught but my own name.'

Mr. Markham gave Mira a little push forward. 'Have you seen my daughter before?'

The landlord, comfortably conscious of the rouleau of guineas residing in his pocket, which the marquess had given him, shook his head. 'Pretty miss, but I ain't seen the likes of her. Don't get ladies here, Your Honor, only gentlemen.'

Mrs. Markham began to sob with relief. 'But was the Marquess of Grantley here?'

demanded Drusilla angrily.

'Now, miss, look about you. Do I look as if I get lords or ladies here?'

'It is most odd,' pursued Mr. Markham, 'that someone should go to such lengths as to forge a document to damn my daughter and pretend it came from you.'

'Probably someone is jealous of her, Your Honor.'

'So that is that,' said Mr. Markham on the road home. 'I am sorry, Mira, for having doubted your word. And we were to attend the Dunsters' ball.'

'We can still go. We will be late and make an entrance,' said Mrs. Markham gaily. She felt almost light-headed with relief.

Drusilla pinched Mira's arm viciously when they were back in the carriage and whispered, 'There is something in this. You have been up to something.'

Mira jerked her arm away but then began to worry about Charles. What if he told Drusilla about finding her returning home in boys' clothes? Mr. Markham might tell him of the landlord's letter, and then Charles would put two and two together. She did so hope the marquess would be at this ball. She had to speak to him about her worries.

When they arrived at the Dunsters' home in Hanover Square, her eyes flew around the ballroom, looking for him. At first she thought with a sinking heart that he was not present,

137

and then with a little sigh of relief, she saw his tall figure at the door to the card room.

Lady Jansen saw Mira arrive and was unable to believe her eyes. She studied the faces of the Markham family for signs of distress, but there were none.

Mira danced with one partner and then another, watching all the time for the marquess. At last he came up to her, and she said hurriedly, 'I must speak to you, my lord. Wait a moment, and I will tell my next partner that I must retire to mend my gown. Then follow me.'

Charles watched jealously as Mira left the room and noticed the way the marquess casually strolled out after her. He was about to follow them when he found Drusilla at his elbow. 'Our waltz, Charles,' she said.

He forced himself to smile as he led her onto the floor. 'I am fatigued,' said Drusilla. 'That wretch Mira!'

'What has she been up to?' asked Charles sharply.

'Papa received a most odd statement supposed to have come from the landlord of an inn near Richmond. In it he claimed to have been host to Mira dressed in boy's clothes and the marquess. They fell in the river and shared a bedchamber while their clothes were drying.'

He stumbled and said, 'And was this true?'

'Not a word,' said Drusilla regretfully. 'But it meant Papa taking us all out to the country to confront this landlord, and that is why we were so late arriving this evening.'

Charles felt vicious pangs of jealousy. Somehow Grantley had squared that landlord. He remembered how shrunken and creased Mira's riding clothes had been. He decided to suffer in silence until the dance was over and then go and try to find the guilty pair.

The marquess joined Mira in the hall, but conscious of all the servants about, he led the way to a small study off the hall. 'We will leave the door open and save our reputations. What happened?'

Mira told him of being found out by Charles but how she had managed to silence him. Then she explained how the landlord of the inn had said he had never sent that document. She ended with, 'But I fear Drusilla will tell Charles about going out to the inn. He will now think it to be true, because he is jealous, because he saw me in riding clothes. I fear he might make a scene.'

'Yes,' said the marquess. 'Where was he when you left the ballroom?'

'Dancing with Drusilla.'

'She will tell him, prompted by jealousy, and he will come looking for you, prompted by jealousy.' He stood frowning. 'It is my intentions toward you that might be brought into question. Very well, we will announce our engagement. You must look as if you adore me.'

'But you don't want to marry me!'

'So you can break the engagement after a decent interval. I am afraid it means you will not find a husband this Season.'

'I have decided I do not want a husband,' said Mira. 'Well, well, Mama will be in alt for the short time in which she believes I am to be a marchioness. How do I look adoring?'

'You like me, do you not?'

'Very much, my lord.'

'Rupert, my name is Rupert.'

'Do I call you Rupert?'

'When we are alone. Otherwise, you address me as Grantley.'

An angry voice could be heard raised in the hall outside, demanding the whereabouts of the Marquess of Grantley.

'Lord Charles,' said the marquess. 'Give me your hand, and look up at me with love in your eyes.'

He took her hand in his. His grasp was strong and comforting.

Charles came striding into the room. The marquess ignored him and gazed down into Mira's green eyes with such an expression of love and tenderness that she stared dizzily back at him.

'What is the meaning of this?' demanded Charles.

The marquess gave him a sweet smile. 'Wish us well, Devere,' he said. 'Miss Mira has done me the inestimable honor of accepting my hand in marriage.'

Charles turned quite white. 'Do Mr. and Mrs. Markham know of this?' he demanded harshly.

'They are about to know of it.' The marquess drew Mira's hand through his arm and gave it a pat. 'I wanted to be sure Mira loved me as much as I love her before approaching her father. Come, my darling.'

He led her out. Charles stood and watched them go. He felt silly now and rather miserable. It did not matter now if Mira had spent the day with the marquess. He was going to marry her, and Mira would be hailed as the success of the Season.

Lady Jansen, watching and watching, saw Mira enter on the marquess's arm. She saw the way he looked down at her, saw the way he led her up to her father and began to speak, saw the look first of bewilderment and then of joy on the faces of Mr. and Mrs. Markham, saw the way Drusilla joined them and how her beautiful face crumpled up with a sour expression.

She felt quite sick with fury. What had gone amiss? Had that package never reached Mr. Markham? She would call on Diggs in the morning. Something must have gone badly wrong. Beside her, Mrs. Anderson, holding her employer's fan, smelling salts, and shawl, allowed herself a little smile of triumph.

Heads were nodding and gossiping. Soon it

was all round the ballroom. Little Mira Markham, the dreadful debutante who had been refused vouchers to Almack's, had not only secured the Marquess of Grantley but it was plain for all to see that the man was madly in love with her.

Lady Jansen might have been relieved to know that Mira Markham was becoming increasingly worried and unhappy. For when the marquess took her in to supper and flirted with her, pressed her hand warmly, and smiled down into her eyes, Mira began to be terrified that she was losing her heart to a man she had agreed to become engaged to only on the condition she canceled that engagement!

CHAPTER SEVEN

'Do you know what I think?' demanded Drusilla, sitting on the end of Mira's bed later that night.

'No, what?' asked Mira sleepily.

'I think there was some truth in that letter supposed to have come from that landlord. I think he had to propose to you to allay a scandal.'

'Go away,' said Mira. 'He loves me and I love him.'

'There was some scandal there, I'll swear,' continued Drusilla, staring down at Mira. 'He

142

can't be interested in a chit like you. Why, you have been the joke of the Season!'

'Go away,' repeated Mira, and she turned on her side and blew out the candle beside the bed.

Drusilla glared at her sulkily and then flounced out.

Mira was immediately awake. She tried to fight down the longing for the engagement to be real, that she and the marquess were not play-acting and their love was real. She reminded herself sternly that she had loved Charles and that had disappeared very quickly. She tried to stop thinking of the marquess, but the bright pictures would not go away—walking in the rain in Covent Garden, riding headlong through the night, playing cards on the floor of the inn, all the shared laughter and adventure.

But who on earth had been behind that statement from the landlord? She had been so very relieved to get away without her escapade's being found out that she had not stopped to wonder who had plotted against her. She must ask the marquess. And she must compose herself and enjoy his company until the end of the Season, when she would live up to her reputation and apparently jilt the best catch on the marriage market. At least her supposed engagement might have brought Charles to his senses, and he could now settle down and be happy with Drusilla. The marquess was to take her driving tomorrow. The day after that his lawyers were to meet her father's lawyers, and the whole matter of dowry and marriage settlements had to be gone into. She felt a stab of guilt. Her father would be very angry with her not only for jilting the marquess but for having caused him unnecessary legal fees. Her mother would feel the family had lost face and be very bitter. But the marquess would think of something. His name was Rupert... Rupert... and murmuring it over and over again like a prayer, she fell asleep.

*   *   *

Lady Jansen walked up the shallow steps to Mr. Diggs's door early the next day and hammered on it ferociously with a gold-topped stick. Silence answered her when she stopped knocking. Then a door opened below, and a querulous woman's voice demanded to know what all the row was about.

Leaning over the banisters, Lady Jansen glared down at a woman still in her undress, an unsavory nightgown covered by an even more unsavory wrapper. 'I am looking for Mr. Diggs,' she called.

'He's left, that's what,' said the woman. 'Packed up and gone, that he has. Left no address neither. Said he wouldn't be coming back for a long time.'

144

Paid off by Grantley and taken my money with him as well, thought Lady Jansen savagely. But there was still hope. She remembered the name of that landlord and the inn. She would go there and see if she could get the truth out of him.

Rain was falling heavily when she arrived at the Green Tree. Perhaps if she had had the wit to try to bribe the landlord, she might have got at the truth, but as it was, his stubborn and oxlike denial that he had ever seen anyone called Mira Markham or the Marquess of Grantley made her call him a liar in front of his customers. He told her roughly to be on her way.

Her brain churned as she was driven back to London. Diggs must have double-crossed her and told the marquess of her intentions and so gained even more money for himself.

She thirsted for revenge. There must be some way she could get even with both of them, for they would now know she was behind the plot to ruin Mira. The marquess would not even look at her. He had ignored her completely at the ball the evening before. She imagined them laughing about her. She arrived home in the worst temper she had ever been in and took her venom out on poor Mrs. Anderson.

But the worm was about to turn. Mrs. Anderson, taking herself shakily out of the room with the excuse that she had some instructions for the cook, suddenly thought of Mira Markham and felt inspired. She, too, should have courage. Such as Mira Markham would not put up with this abuse. There were other ladies in London who might engage her as companion.

It was then that she thought of the Marquess of Grantley. He owed her a favor. Other people in the past had owed Mrs. Anderson favors, but she had never claimed any of them. But this was one she was going to claim. The dream of handing her resignation to her vindictive employer buoyed her spirits up for the rest of the day.

*   *   *

Mira felt guilty when both her parents actually escorted her down to the hall to wave goodbye to her when she left to go driving with the marquess. She was suddenly so shy of him that she could not return any of his loverlike glances, although, despite her shyness, she felt a nagging irritation that he should prove to be such a good actor.

London was sunny and warm. Two young misses with their maids passed on the street, muslin dresses and long, fringed shawls fluttering in the wind. They looked up enviously at Mira as she sat in the high-perch phaeton.

Mira waved to her parents and then

muttered to the marquess, 'I feel like a fraud.'

'Don't,' he admonished as they drove off. 'We are in love, the day is sunny, and you are the happiest lady in London.'

'Who was responsible for finding out about us?' asked Mira.

'Lady Jansen. She hired an ex-Runner called Diggs to follow us. She thought we were having an affair.'

'That woman again! Why?'

'I believe she thought that had she proof of this supposed affair, then you would be sent home and I might marry her.'

'Just wait until I see her again!'

His voice was severe. 'You will ignore her, Mira. Making a scene might make people ask her what it was all about, and then they might begin to believe her story.'

'So how did you put a stop to it?'

'I bribed the landlord of the Green Tree heavily to forget he ever saw us. I visited Diggs and told him I would pay him handsomely to leave town for a healthy period. If he did not, I said I would make sure he was never employed again. But your worries are over. My intentions are so obviously honorable that no scandal can stick to us now. When do you plan to jilt me?'

'At the end of the Season. Oh, Rupert, as to that, I will be in the suds for throwing away the best catch on the marriage market.'

'Do not worry—toward the end of the Season I shall be seen in public with a mistress.

I shall behave so badly that your parents will damn me and praise you for having the courage to get rid of me.'

'And . . . and you will not mind?'

'Not I.'

'You will . . . you will take a mistress?'

'I shall probably engage the willing services of some pretty opera dancer only for the time it will take to show the world that I am a dreadful person.'

'But surely that will ruin *your* chances of marriage?'

'By next Season the matchmaking mamas will have deliberately forgotten about it. I am rich; I have a title.'

'And that's the way of the world.' Mira sighed.

'We are approaching the Park, and you are supposed to look radiant. Smile!'

She smiled up at him from under the brim of her jaunty straw hat, and he looked down at her with such loving tenderness that she said shakily, 'You do that indecently well, my lord.'

'Rupert,' he corrected. 'I am quite fond of you, my chuck, so it comes easily to me.'

She drew a little comfort from this tepid affection and managed to look as happy as she was supposed to be.

Drusilla, being driven by Charles, saw how all eyes were turned to her little sister, saw the envious glances, and felt she almost hated Mira. What was it about Mira? She looked the

148

same, apart from the fact that she was modishly dressed. She had the same odd high cheekbones, the same frizzy hair, and she was much too slim to be fashionable. As their carriage came alongside that of the marquess, Mira smiled and bowed, but the marquess was looking at Mira with such a *doting* expression on his face that he did not appear to notice either Charles or Drusilla.

'I am surprised,' said Charles in a flat voice as he drove on. 'That is a love match if ever there was one.'

'He does not know what Mira is really like,' said Drusilla, two spots of angry color on her cheeks.

'I do not think any of us appreciated Mira's qualities enough,' said Charles sadly.

'Qualities! What qualities?'

'Humor, gaiety, kindness, and beauty.'

Drusilla fanned herself rapidly. 'Let us discuss our future, Charles. Have you written to your regiment?'

'As to that, I have decided not to sell out.'

'What! What of me? I do not want to be an army wife!'

'I am sorry about that.' He folded his lips in a firm line and stared straight ahead.

'I cannot go with you to a barracks. I am too delicate. What if you go to war?'

And then he said those words that ended the engagement: 'Mira would follow her husband anywhere.'

'Take me home,' said Drusilla in an even voice, 'so that we may tell my parents the engagement is finished.'

'As you wish,' he said with seeming indifference.

Drusilla felt her comforting world of adoring and admiring people collapsing about her ears. She sat in silence all the way home, her back ramrod straight, her face rigid.

They walked together up to the drawing room.

Mr. and Mrs. Markham were both there.

'Papa,' said Drusilla, 'our engagement is over. Charles insists on staying in the army.'

'What is this nonsense?' cried Mr. Markham, springing to his feet.

'Furthermore,' went on Drusilla, 'I cannot measure up to such a paragon as Mira.' She suddenly burst into tears and fled the room.

Mr. Markham settled down to try to salvage the engagement. In a calmer voice he pleaded that engaged couples were often subject to nerves. But it slowly dawned on him that Charles desperately wanted the engagement to be at an end. There was nothing he could do but agree to it.

When Charles had left, he turned sadly to his wife. 'Now we are suffering for our cruelty to Mira.'

'Cruelty? What can you mean, Mr. Markham?'

'We have sadly indulged Drusilla while

ignoring Mira. As a result Mira has developed qualities of strength and character that Drusilla lacks. Drusilla has always relied only on her beauty. At least Mira has done well for herself, and Drusilla is still exceptionally beautiful, so she will soon find a new suitor.'

But it never dawned on either of the Markham parents to go and comfort Drusilla.

When Mira returned, they smiled on her, asked her if she had enjoyed her drive, and smiled again when she said, 'Very much.'

'We have sad news,' said Mr. Markham. 'Drusilla has broken off her engagement with Charles.'

'Why?'

'Charles refuses to sell out.'

'And is Drusilla content with the breaking of the engagement?'

'She left the room in tears, but she will come about. She will soon find another suitor.'

Mira turned, ran upstairs, and went to Drusilla's room, where she found that young lady facedown on the bed, crying her eyes out.

'Now then,' said Mira, climbing onto the bed and gathering her weeping sister into her arms, 'what is all this about?'

'It's ... it's all y-your f-fault,' sobbed Drusilla. 'You took him away from me.'

'That is fustian, you goose, and you know it. Charles has always loved the army.'

'H-he should love me m-more!'

'But you never loved him, Drusilla. You

151

became engaged to him only to spite me.'

'How did you know that?' said Drusilla in naive amazement. She sat up and dried her eyes.

'It's the sort of thing you would do, sis. So why are you upset?'

'I was looking forward to being married,' said Drusilla. 'I felt I was so successful, the first debutante at the Season to be engaged. And Charles is so suitable and so handsome. What am I to do? Everyone will laugh at me.'

'Listen widgeon, everyone will know you broke the engagement, so why will they laugh? The gentlemen will crowd round you again, and you will be the belle of the ball. The only reason you have not been the belle of the ball recently is that you have been engaged.'

'Do you think so?'

'I know so. You must show Charles, too, what he has lost. You must have everyone talking about how kind and charming you are instead of just talking about your beauty. When poor little Mr. Andrews danced with you, you looked every bit as contemptuous of him as you obviously felt. You must be kind to all. Only think how you are hurting now. Other people hurt just as much as you, Drusilla. And you will not look at all beautiful at Vauxhall tonight with red eyes.'

'I *cannot* go to Vauxhall,' wailed Drusilla. 'Charles is to escort us.'

'Then you must start right away. You must

be easy and friendly with Charles and tell him on calmer reflection that you are sorry you ever asked him to leave the army.' And I, thought Mira grimly, will look so much in love with Rupert that it should crush any warm feelings Charles might still hold for me.

'Why are you bothering about me?' asked Drusilla. 'I have always been nasty to you.'

'We are sisters.'

'So we are,' said Drusilla. 'You must advise me on my gown, Mira.'

For Mira it seemed strange to be able to chat easily with her sister as they looked at gowns, gloves, and stoles to put together the most attractive ensemble.

They entered the drawing room together at nine o'clock that evening, both in white muslin with light pelisses over their gowns. Mira was wearing one of the new fashionable Turkish turbans, and Drusilla was wearing a little Juliet cap frosted with silver sequins on her glossy brown hair. Mira immediately went over to the marquess, linked arms with him, and smiled up adoringly into his face while he covered her hand with his own. Drusilla, to her parents' amazement, prattled easily to Charles as if nothing had happened. It was the usual Drusilla conversation about gloves and gowns, but there were a new vulnerability and softness about her that enhanced her beauty.

The marquess thought about the strange visit he had had from Mrs. Anderson before he left. The faded spinster had quite strongly pointed out to him that it was his duty to help her, and half-exasperated, half-amused, he had sent her to his mother with a strong letter of recommendation.

Charles was beginning to relax and enjoy himself as they neared the pleasure gardens of Vauxhall by way of Westminster Bridge. The night was calm and clear with a full moon, and as they approached, they could hear the orchestra playing. They were not a fashionable party in that they had arrived in time to watch the performers and see the fireworks display. The high sticklers came after midnight, claiming that they were not entertained by 'childish amusements'.

It was Mira's first visit to Vauxhall, and she was delighted with it all—from the tree-lined walks with their many lanterns to the orchestra playing in the cockle-shaped bandstand.

They had supper in a box and made a cheerful party. Mira was out to forget that her engagement was a sham. As she was falling deeper and deeper in love with the marquess by the minute, it was all too easy to flirt with him.

After supper the marquess said he would take Mira to see the fireworks display, and Charles, after a hesitation, said he would escort Drusilla.

Drusilla waited until they were well away from the box and then said quietly to Charles,

'I owe you an apology.'

'For breaking our engagement? Think nothing of it.'

'Not that,' Drusilla tried to remember what Mira had told her to say. A little of the old resentment against Mira rose up in her brain and then fizzled and died. 'I should not have asked you to sell out. I have always known you love your army life.' She gave a light laugh. 'You have had a lucky escape, Charles. And you are quite right—someone like Mira would make you a more suitable bride.'

This was said without any rancor. There was nothing in the way she said it to make him feel guilty. All about him on the walk, men were stopping to stare at Drusilla. He had not quite been aware in the last week or two what a stir her beauty caused. He did not even have his longing for Mira to take his mind off the broken engagement, for he found it almost impossible to think romantically of a young lady who so obviously doted on another—and quite vulgarly, too, he thought, looking ahead to where Mira was hanging on her marquess's arm and gazing up into his face.

So he said quietly, 'I do love my army life, but I have an apology to make as well. I should not have compared you to your sister. You are both charming in different ways. Do say you will forgive me.'

'Of course, Charles,' said Drusilla lightly. 'We have known each other for so long that it would be silly to quarrel now.'

'Do you like fireworks displays?'

Only the day before Drusilla would have said coldly that she considered fireworks displays tiresome because that was what it was fashionable to say. But by copying Mira's honesty, she hoped to gain some of her sister's appeal. And so she said, 'I *adore* fireworks displays. I will ooh and aah and clap my hands, and you will consider me a country bumpkin.'

'I have never seen anyone less like a country bumpkin,' said Charles. 'We will oooh and aaah and be children together.'

But it was Mira who jumped up and down and hailed every burst of stars above her head with delight.

'You are a rowdy child,' said the marquess after the show was over.

'I am not a child, Rupert.'

'You behave like a child.'

Her eyes flirted up at him. 'Do you kiss children, Rupert? Fie, for shame!'

He laughed and steered her off the walk and into the darkness of a glade. 'No, I kiss minxes—like this.'

He tilted up her chin. She felt she should stop him, that she was drowning in emotion. She saw his lips descending and closed her eyes. As his mouth closed over her own, she felt her senses reeling. A tide of red, raw passion seemed to start in the pit of her stomach and swell up to her lips.

He at last released her and looked down at her in dazed amazement. 'Mira!'

She stared up at him in the darkness, tears glittering in her eyes. 'You are wicked, Rupert, *wicked.*' And she turned and ran away.

He was so startled, he stood there for a long moment before going in pursuit of her.

* * *

Charles and Drusilla walked back, arm in arm. 'So when do you leave us, Charles?' asked Drusilla, still striving to keep her tone light.

'I shall wait until the end of the Season. It is such a long time since I have had any leave. I plan to enjoy it.'

'You will have all the fun of observing me trying to ensnare a suitable gentleman,' said Drusilla. 'How tiresome it all is. It is a pity Mira is engaged, or we might have agreed to remain spinsters.'

'You are not meant to be a spinster. But you, Drusilla, are certainly not meant to be an army wife.'

'I never asked enough questions about that,' said Drusilla. 'What is it really like?'

'We have a great deal of fun. There are balls and parties, just like in civilian life. We are based in Dover at the moment, as you know. Of course, I would not have expected you to live in barracks were we married, nor would my commanding officer. We should have taken

157

a trim house in town and entertained until such time as my regiment was moved on again. Some of the officers' wives do not join them, but stay at home and endure the long separations.'

Drusilla sighed. 'Perhaps that sort of life might be better than facing up to the fact that I have to allow myself to be courted by some gentleman I really do not know very well. Spinsters, poor things, are so despised. It is not fair!'

Charles steered her around three gentlemen who had come to a standstill to stare at her beauty. His thoughts were beginning to race. This was a different Drusilla. He had been hard on her. He had sorely misjudged her.

'Drusilla,' he said abruptly, 'step aside from the walk with me. I think we need to talk further.'

'About what, Charles?' she asked, but she allowed him to lead her from the walk and into the same glade in which the marquess had so lately stood with Mira.

'I feel I owe you an explanation about Mira.'

'That is not necessary,' said Drusilla, turning her face away.

'I was very fond of Mira when she was a child. I was briefly attracted to her, but that is over. Mira and I would never have suited.'

'You say that only because she is spoony about Grantley and no longer available!'

This was only the truth, but Charles

suddenly did not want Drusilla to know that.

'That is not true! I think we made a very bad start. Drusilla, why do we not try again—but I shall not sell out.'

Her relief was immense. She had been dreading the rest of the Season, possibly ending up married to some 'suitable' man she did not really know. Charles was handsome and kind. She should not give in so easily, but she found herself saying weakly, 'Yes, Charles.'

He kissed her gently and chastely on the lips, and then together they moved out of the glade, Charles once more experiencing all the old joy of the attention his beautiful partner was attracting, and Drusilla weak with relief that the engagement was back on.

*   *   *

Mira sat in the box, face white, green eyes glittering with unshed tears. 'This is ridiculous!' cried Mr. Markham. 'It cannot be off. We have sent a notice of your engagement to the newspapers along with the notice of the cancellation of Drusilla's engagement. Oh, here is Grantley. My lord, I cannot believe this. Mira tells me the engagement is at an end.'

The marquess's face was a polite mask. Underneath it he was furious with Mira. He had gone out of his way to help her, and she had repaid him by behaving in this infuriating way, kissing him with a passion he had never experienced before and then running away from him. He was sick of the Markham family. He was sick of the whole thing.

'If that is what Mira wants,' he said evenly, 'then allow me to inform the newspapers of the cancellation.'

'But can we not discuss this?' wailed Mrs. Markham.

The marquess got to his feet and made an elaborate bow. 'There is nothing to discuss. You shall not be seeing me again. I plan to go to the country. I am not feeling well and wish to return home. Good night!'

He leapt over the edge of the box and walked away into the night.

Before the Markhams could berate Mira, Charles and Drusilla walked up to the box.

'We are still engaged,' said Drusilla sunnily.

'You cannot be,' said the outraged Mr. Markham. 'There will be a notice in the newspapers tomorrow canceling your engagement!'

'Then I suggest we put one in the day after to say it is still on,' said Charles with a laugh.

That was when Mrs. Markham fainted.

*   *   *

The following day Lady Jansen listened in grim silence as Mrs. Anderson handed in her notice and made the most of it, telling Lady Jansen in her prim voice exactly what she had always thought of her.

'And just where are you going?' demanded Lady Jansen when she could get a word in edgewise.

'I am to be companion to the Dowager Duchess of Grantley.'

It was only when her companion had left and her amazement at the turning of the worm, which had kept her nearly speechless, had begun to ebb that Lady Jansen's brain began to work at a great rate. Grantley! Now she was sure she knew how the marquess had found out about Diggs, about herself, and about the Green Tree, and had managed to spike her guns.

Her thoughts returned to the landlord, and she struck her fist on the table beside her, sending a Dresden ornament flying. What a fool she had been. If the man had taken a bribe for his silence, all she had to do was offer him a heavier bribe to speak up.

She called for her carriage and then went to change her clothes. She then called at her bank and drew out a sum of money in gold guineas before setting out once more for the Green Tree.

At first the landlord stood by his story. But when she looked round and saw the tap was empty, Lady Jansen opened a wash leather bag of gold and spilled the contents onto the table. 'I know Grantley paid you to keep your mouth shut, but I am prepared to pay you handsomely

161

to tell what really happened.'

His eyes gleamed at the sight of the gold. 'You would only be telling the truth,' urged Lady Jansen.

'Reckon it depends on what I would have to do.'

'All you would have to do is come with me to a Mr. and Mrs. Markham and tell your story. Then my carriage will return you here. You would not have to write anything or appear in court. Simply tell your story. Wait a bit. You must tell it twice. First to a Mrs. Gardener and then to the Markhams. Look at the gold, man. It is enough to keep such as you for the rest of your life.'

'But even if there's no court business, what if this Grantley comes after me with a horsewhip or a gun?'

'After all this is in the open, he would not dare.'

'Reckon I'll earn my money then,' said the landlord, taking off his baize apron. 'I'll just tell the wife to take over here.'

CHAPTER EIGHT

For some reason he could not quite explain, the angry marquess decided to delay his journey home to the country until the end of the week. Like any other aristocrat he was

162

never much given to introspection, and so he did not know that his new anger at and dislike of Mira were prompted by nothing more than wounded pride. He, the catch of the Season, had been jilted by a hoyden. The fact that the engagement was meant to end anyway did not occur to his angry brain.

He would go to the opera that night and to the ball afterward, flirt with all the pretty girls, and get the world to think that it was really he who had decided the engagement was wrong. That his kiss had been returned with the sort of passion that had been entirely new to him was something he refused to think about. All he knew was that he was very unhappy and very angry and that it was all Mira's fault.

He did not consider for a moment that Mira might feel devastated, but that was what she did feel. Only the idea of the hell it might be to continue with a pretend engagement to a man with whom she had fallen suddenly and deeply in love made her endure the present hell of her parents' disapproval and disappointment. Drusilla, grateful for Mira's help and advice, and comfortably happy now that her own engagement was a reality again, tried to comfort her young sister, but not being in love herself or having any conception of the turbulent emotions that gripped Mira, she could only offer platitudes such as 'By your next Season everyone will have forgotten about it.' This was no comfort to Mira, who did not really care whether society forgot about it or not and realized only that she herself never could and never would.

But to her relief Drusilla did suggest something practical: that Mira accompany her and Charles on a drive. Neither referred to the broken engagement, and Mira was only too glad to escape the house and the tremendous weight of disapproval of her that seemed to permeate every room like a thick fog. By the time they returned, Mira was beginning to feel more courageous. The marquess would not be angry with her. He could not be. All she had done was end the engagement sooner than she had said she would end it. And so she avoided contemplating the fact that in society's eyes, the cancellation of an engagement by a young miss after one day—which is what it would appear between the announcement in the newspapers and the subsequent announcement of the cancellation—would cause a furor of gossip.

Had she had any inkling of what was about to break over her head, she would have fled to the country.

*　　*　　*

Mira had not seen her father or mother when she had returned from the drive with Charles and Drusilla. The butler said they were receiving visitors in the Yellow Saloon. Had

Mira not been so preoccupied with her troubles, she would have stopped to wonder why her parents considered the damp and little-used Yellow Saloon suitable for visitors.

In the Yellow Saloon Mrs. Markham looked like a rabbit confronted by a snake and reached blindly for the comfort of her husband's hand. Twisting his hat between his fingers and standing behind Lady Jansen's chair, the landlord, Giles Brand, described in the tones of a good child repeating a well-learned lesson that afternoon at the inn when Mira and the marquess had fallen into the river, booked his best bedchamber to remove their clothes, and had spent the time wrapped in blankets, playing cards.

Mr. Markham found his voice. 'Look here, fellow, you don't know my daughter. How did you know it was my daughter? You told me you had never seen her before!'

Lady Jansen had been too stupid to see what might come out of it and was too late to stop Mr. Brand from saying guilelessly, 'Well, you see, my lady here, she hired an ex-Runner, Diggs, to find out about them, but that-there Marquess of Grantley, he called and told me to keep my mouth shut, but then Lady Jansen told me as how I ought to tell the truth.'

'So,' said Mr. Markham bitterly, 'you were probably paid by this Diggs, then paid by Grantley, and probably paid again by this dreadful person here.'

'Remember to whom you speak,' said Lady Jansen haughtily.

'People like you, madam, are scum, are as dirt beneath my boots,' raged Mr. Markham. 'Get out of here, and take your paid creature with you.'

Lady Jansen swept out with the landlord, her head held high, but her stomach was churning as she suddenly realized that she was about to be more socially damned than Mira Markham. Such as Mrs. Gardener might gossip, but the ton would be shocked rigid by a lady who had gone to such lengths as to hire an ex-Runner to ruin a debutante. What might she find out about them if she put her mind to it!

When they had left, Mr. Markham turned to his wife, who was quietly weeping. 'Dry your tears,' he said harshly. 'There is no time for tears. There must be a way to save that wretched girl from ruin.' He rang the bell and told the footman who answered it to take a note to the Marquess of Grantley, summoning him urgently.

'We must speak to Mira,' whispered Mrs. Markham.

'Oh, no,' said Mr. Markham. 'I do not want to listen to her lies and evasions. I now believe that story about her going with Grantley as his tiger on a curricle race.'

They waited and waited. Mrs. Markham was silently praying that it would all turn out to be lies on the part of Lady Jansen. Only one little ray of comfort lightened her darkness. Dear Drusilla was engaged again. Drusilla always behaved just as she ought.

And then the marquess was announced. He stood in the doorway, and one look at their faces told them that somehow his escapade with Mira had been discovered.

'Sit down, Grantley,' said Mr. Markham quietly, for he was now beyond rage.

The marquess listened with a grim face while Mr. Markham told him of Lady Jansen's visit. 'You have ruined our daughter,' ended Mr. Markham wearily. 'I cannot understand how a gentleman of your rank and breeding should have behaved so badly, so cruelly.'

'Well, there is only one solution,' said the marquess.

'I see no solution.'

'Mira will just need to marry me after all. The whole idea of the engagement was initially to scotch any gossip. Love and marriage make the escapade romantic. I suggest you inform everyone, as I shall, that it was probably the malicious Lady Jansen who sent the notice of the cancellation of the engagement to the newspapers.'

A glimmer of hope began to light up Mr. Markham's eyes.

He rang the bell and ordered the footman to bring Mira down to them. Mira appeared, already dressed in an opera gown of gold damask. Her eyes flew from the marquess to her parents.

She sat down on the edge of a chair and listened in increasing horror to the tale of the scandal about her day with the marquess. The only comfort she could hang on to was that she would be banished to the country and leave wicked London and one heartbreaker behind.

'You have both behaved disgracefully,' said Mr. Markham sternly, 'but there is one solution to this.'

'I am to leave London?'

'No, Grantley is to do the honorable thing. You will marry him. We will tell everyone that the cancellation of the engagement—it is too late to get the notice removed—was actually probably another evil trick of Lady Jansen's.'

Mira went quite white. 'I cannot marry Grantley.'

'You have no say in the matter. You will come with us to the opera, and both of you will present a united and happy front to the world.'

Mira's green eyes looked pleadingly at the marquess. 'Don't you see, they are *forcing* you to marry me!'

'Exactly,' said the marquess maliciously. In a perverse way he was beginning to enjoy himself. He did not stop to wonder why he was not in the slightest dismayed at the prospect of marriage to Mira. She had sorely dented his pride, and he felt he was getting even.

Courage, thought Mira. I must have

courage. She turned to her father. 'May I have a few words in private with Grantley?'

Mr. Markham rose and held out his hand to his wife. 'Come, Mrs. Markham, we shall allow them ten minutes.'

Mr. and Mrs. Markham left, leaving the door punctiliously open.

'You don't want to marry me,' said Mira fiercely as soon as they were alone.

'May I remind you, my sweeting, that it was you who canceled the engagement? I have to marry you.' He added piously, 'It is my duty.'

'Why should you, who could marry any female in society, want to marry me? Be sensible. If you refuse, I will be sent to the country, out of this horrible world of malice and gossip, and I can be free with my horse and dogs.'

He shook his head. 'I contributed to your downfall by encouraging you to behave badly. You must take the consequences.'

She looked at him with a little hope in her eyes. 'It could be a marriage of convenience, I mean, a marriage in name only.'

'Oh, no, I want children, lots and lots of them, Mira.'

She twisted a handkerchief in her hands. 'What am I to do?'

'May I point out that you have made your bed, and you are just going to have to lie on it and try to enjoy it.'

'You are being crude and vulgar!'

169

'You have no idea how crude and vulgar I mean to be. So we must return to our role as a supremely happy couple. You could start by kissing me.'

'Never!'

He crossed the room to where she sat and knelt down in front of her. He took her face firmly between his hands. 'What's in a kiss, Mira? You kiss most delightfully.'

'I d-don't w-want to kiss you.'

'Then I will kiss you.'

He closed his lips over hers. She primmed her lips in a firm line, but his mouth worked seductively on her own until he felt her bosom rise and fall and her lips finally soften. He was just beginning to feel her response when Mr. Markham's voice sounded in his ears. 'I shall return in a few moments, which should give you enough time to compose yourselves and behave in a more seemly manner.'

The marquess stood up and held out his hand. 'Come, Mira, you are tied to me for life, and so you will need to start to accept that fact. We have caused your parents great distress. Make them happy by at least pretending to be in love with me. It is no use sulking and raging. You are trapped.'

When Mr. and Mrs. Markham entered, they were standing hand in hand. Mira's face was pink where it had been white only such a short time ago.

'You may go abovestairs and tell Drusilla we

will be ready to leave in an hour,' said Mr. Markham. 'Mrs. Markham and I still have to change and dress. Charles is already waiting in the drawing room for us.'

The marquess indicated his own dress clothes. 'I will stay and accompany you as well,' he said.

'As you will,' said Mr. Markham frostily. 'Mira—go!'

Glad to escape, Mira ran up the stairs to find Drusilla waiting for her. 'What is this?' cried Drusilla, all round-eyed with wonder. 'Mama told me some garbled story about how you were ruined because all that tale of your sharing a bedroom with Grantley was true. Did you actually do . . . well . . . *that*? What was it like?'

'No, I didn't do *that*,' said Mira. 'We only played cards as we waited for our clothes to dry, and now I've got to marry him.'

'I do not understand you, Mira. At first it looked as if you were delighted at the prospect of marrying him, and the next minute you are breaking off the engagement, and now you look as if you are attending your own funeral because it is on again. Grantley is rich, handsome, and titled. You will be a marchioness. Think on that!'

'He will break my heart,' said Mira wearily. 'I am in love with him.'

Drusilla stared at her sister with a puzzled frown on her forehead. 'And he appears to be in love with you, so what's the rub?'

'He is only pretending to love me so as to make it all look so respectable. I can imagine nothing more hellish—'

'Mira! Your *language*!'

'... hellish,' continued Mira firmly, 'than being married to a man who does not love me.'

'But you will not need to see much of him. Gentlemen, or so I have observed, spend much of their lives in sports or in their clubs.'

'I will need to give him children!'

Drusilla turned her face away and said in a low voice, 'How does one do that, Mira?'

'I do not know,' said Mira, 'but I only know it involves a lot of kissing, and when he kisses me, he takes my soul away.'

'Oh, that's vastly pretty,' said Drusilla appreciatively. 'I read a line like that in a romance once. But you are living in a dream world, Mira. You are fantasizing.'

'Impossible! Impossible to talk to you,' said Mira. 'Come, we must join the gentlemen in the drawing room.' She put her arm around Drusilla's waist. 'You mean well, dear sis, but it is like trying to play a piece of sweet music to the tone-deaf.'

Charles and the marquess rose to greet them as they entered the drawing room. The marquess went straight to Mira, took her hand, and kissed it.

'This is a shameful business,' said Charles heavily.

The marquess turned and looked him up and down, then said evenly, 'Any more impertinent observations like that and I shall feel obliged to call you out.'

'Play something for us, Drusilla,' said Mira hurriedly.

Drusilla sat down at the harp, and her fingers rippled expertly over the strings. Charles stood near her to admire the pretty picture she made.

The marquess sat down on the sofa, and Mira sat primly beside him. 'You do not look adoring enough,' he commented.

'How can I look adoring when I am forcing a man to marry me?'

'If I can accept it with good grace, then so can you.'

For one brief little moment Mira had had the mad hope that he might say, 'I love you,' but all he had done was to underline the fact that he was entering a marriage he didn't want.

*   *   *

At the opera Mira was conscious of all the staring eyes and whispering voices. She felt naked. The marquess pressed her hand and whispered. 'Courage,' and she did her best to look happy when all she wanted was to escape and put as much distance as possible between herself and him. But on the whole she behaved very well—until the ball after the opera.

The first dance with her was claimed by young Mr. Danby, who wished her well and hoped she would be happy. Mira was aware of the marquess watching them, and some imp prompted her to flirt with Mr. Danby. The marquess turned away from the scene with seeming indifference but promptly took a pretty young lady onto the floor and began to pay her a great deal of attention. Mira, wondering whether it was possible to die from sheer jealousy, continued to flirt outrageously with partner after partner, while the marquess, for his part, appeared to be trying to outdo her. She had promised him the supper dance, and so they finally went into the refreshment room together, both with angry eyes as hard as diamonds.

'Just what the deuce do you think you are playing at?' demanded the marquess.

'I do not know what you mean,' said Mira huffily.

'You are behaving like the veriest trollop.'

'How dare you!'

'I dare. And when we are married, miss, you will behave just as you ought.'

'You were the one who encouraged me in this folly.'

'And I am graciously getting you out of the consequences of a folly in which you were a willing partner.'

Mira glared at him. 'And what is so gracious about flirting vulgarly with every woman in the

174

room?'

'I have not yet got around to every woman in the room. But I shall. Be assured of that, my sweeting.'

'I wish I had never met you,' muttered Mira.

'Oh. I do wish you would stop whining and try to behave like a lady.' The marquess's tone was glacial.

Almost beside herself with rage, jealousy, and hurt, Mira slapped his face, and the marquess promptly slapped her back. People stopped eating; people stopped talking. For one long moment the silence in the supper room was absolute.

Then Drusilla, prompted for about the first time in her life by the thought of helping someone else, said in a loud voice, 'I think this meat is bad, Charles. It has a peculiar taste.'

Voices rose all around discussing the meat.

'You struck me,' said Mira. 'Gentlemen do not strike ladies.'

'The provocation was great. You hit me first. Was I to allow myself to be humiliated in public and take it with a smile?'

'Well, I am sorry I forgot myself,' said Mira. She looked so lost and miserable that he said in a gentle voice, 'Do eat something. It is not like you to pick at your food. Now we will get a roasting from your father. Perhaps we are well suited after all, Mira. I have never known two people to behave so badly in public. The only way we will now save face is to look so madly in

175

love that people will put it down to a lovers' quarrel. Come, Mira, if you will not do it for me or yourself, do it for your shattered parents.' He raised her hand to his lips and kissed it.

Mira saw the wisdom of his words and forced herself to play the part of a happy girl again, delighted with her partner.

But although they both behaved admirably for the rest of the evening, the marquess was not at all surprised when Mr. Markham, on their arrival back at St. James's Square, told him to step indoors with them.

'I will see you and Mira alone,' he said, opening the door of the Yellow Saloon.

'Can you both explain the meaning of your disgraceful behavior this evening?' began Mr. Markham.

The truth was that both of them had been driven mad by jealousy, but neither was going to admit that. The marquess, who had never felt so much in the wrong in his well-ordered life before, fought down his rising irritation.

'We are both a trifle overwrought,' he said easily.

'I am alarmed by the pair of you,' pursued Mr. Markham. 'I do not want to know what really happened in that inn, but you are going on in public like lovers. Therefore, Grantley, I must suggest you get a special license and that you and Mira marry as soon as possible.'

'Mira is not pregnant,' said the marquess

bluntly.

'So you say.' Mr. Markham stood his ground. 'You would not say and Mira would not know. I repeat, you must marry as quickly as possible.'

'Oh, very well.' The marquess sighed. 'May as well get it over with. But your daughter is still a virgin.'

Mira thought she could not hurt anymore, but his cold words, 'May as well get it over with,' cut her to the quick.

'Papa,' she begged, 'send me back home. I do not want to marry. I want to remain a spinster.'

Her father's eyes were as cold as ice. 'You will do exactly as you are told from now on. You are a great disappointment to me, Mira.'

The marquess saw the tears start in Mira's eyes and said furiously, 'That is nothing new. She always was. You wanted a son, so in order to get your attention, she tried to behave like a boy. Did you try to stop it? No, it amused you, and you and your wife were too wrapped up in the beautiful Drusilla to care. So do not sneer at her. Yes, I behaved badly, but do not blame Mira for a standard of behavior that is entirely of your making. Now I will bid you both good night. I will call on the bishop tomorrow and obtain a special license.'

He strode out of the room.

'Mira ...' began Mr. Markham, but she stood up and walked to the door. 'No, Papa,' she said. 'No more.'

'You will be locked in your room until you come to your senses,' he shouted after her.

Drusilla, standing on the first landing, heard that. She saw Mira stumble blindly past her and heard her father ordering a footman to go up to Miss Mira's room, to lock the door behind her and bring him the key.

It's nothing really to do with me, thought Drusilla. And yet she could not help remembering the way Mira had come to *her* when she was in distress. It was thanks to Mira that she, Drusilla, was now comfortably engaged to Charles. She went to her own room and sat and worried, hearing the house about her fall silent as everyone went to bed.

At last she went downstairs quietly to a room off the servants' hall where she knew the spare keys were to be found. Holding a candle high, she studied the attached labels, finally selecting the one to Mira's room. Then she darted back upstairs and softly opened the door.

Mira was not crying. She was slumped in a chair by the window, still in her opera gown, staring blindly ahead.

'Mira,' said Drusilla, 'what happened this evening? You behaved so badly and Grantley slapped you, right in front of everyone.'

'He was flirting with all the pretty ladies, Drusilla,' said Mira, 'and I was so jealous, I could not bear it.'

'It could have been because you were flirting quite dreadfully yourself, Mira.'

'That's different,' said Mira mulishly. 'And now Papa thinks something ... awful ... happened between us at that inn, and he has ordered Grantley to get a special license and marry me as soon as possible, and he, Grantley, said he "may as well get it over with". He doesn't love me, sis, and he never will.'

'Oh, I don't understand!' wailed Drusilla. 'Why can't you be comfortable?'

'Because I love him but he doesn't love me, and I cannot bear it. I am going to run away.'

'Where?'

'I will go home and be by myself, and he will be so furious, he will refuse to marry me.'

'Oh, Mira, home will be cold and empty, with only Mr. George, the caretaker, and his wife in residence.'

'I do not care. I shall run mad if I stay here.'

'But how will you travel?'

'By stage. I have my pin money.'

'When they find you gone, they will blame me, Mira, for bringing you the key.'

'I shall replace the key before I leave. No one will ever know you took it.'

Drusilla sat down weakly on the bed. 'Could you not wait until you see Grantley again and tell him of your love?'

'Never! And you are not to tell anyone where I am, Drusilla. Not even Charles.

Promise.'

'Yes, yes,' said Drusilla. 'Is there nothing I can say or do to stop you?'

'No, give me a hug'—Mira rose wearily to her feet—'and then leave me to my devices.'

Drusilla embraced her and then went to her own room, feeling puzzled and upset. She did hope madness did not run in the family, but that was the only explanation she could think of for Mira's wild behavior.

Mira looked at her own boy's clothes, thinking as she did so that she had never confessed to the marquess that the riding clothes he had lent her were now buried in the garden. She took off her opera gown and dressed in her masculine garb. Her hat was gone, lost in the river, but there were old hats in a closet off the hall. She put some items into a canvas bag and slung it over her shoulder, blew out the candles, locked the door behind her, and made her way quietly down the stairs. She replaced the spare key and then mounted the stairs to the front hall. She slid back the heavy bolts, reflecting that her father would be furious that she had gone and left the front door unlocked.

She ran across St. James's Square and headed for the City on foot. Dawn was brightening the sky as she reached the Strand. How marvelous it had been that day he had driven her along here. Down Fleet Street and up Ludgate Hill she hurried and so to the Belle

Sauvage Inn in time to catch the stage.

As London gradually fell behind her and the sun rose on a perfect summer's day, despite the heaviness of her heart, she felt she had done the right thing. He would be shot of her at last, and somehow, some year, her father might forgive her.

*   *   *

Mira's disappearance was not discovered until eleven o'clock. Drusilla had risen early for her and had suddenly felt she could not bear the strain of waiting for the storm to break any longer. So she had roused her parents and said she had been calling to Mira through the door of her room and could not get an answer. Mr. Markham rang the bell and ordered a footman to unlock the door of Miss Mira's bedchamber.

The footman returned in a rush to say that Miss Mira had gone.

Mr. Markham swore an oath his frightened wife and daughter had never heard him use before. Shouting for his valet, shouting for his carriage to be brought round, shouting at the unfairness of the world at large and swearing that Mira would be found at Grantley's because 'that disgraceful pair cannot keep their hands off each other,' he soon set out for Grosvenor Square.

He was met by the marquess's furious denials and worse than that. The enraged marquess said that Mira had added insult to injury by broadcasting to the world that she would rather run away from home than have anything to do with him. He was sick of her and sick of the Markhams. He had no intention now of marrying her. He then ordered the stricken Mr. Markham from his house.

After Lord Charles had been summoned, a council of war was held in the drawing room of St. James's Square. The disgrace Mira had brought on the family was too much to bear. Charles would understand that they must take Drusilla home. He said he would return to the country himself. Drusilla, who did not want to leave London, protested in vain. So deep was Mr. Markham's shame that he ordered the shutters to remain closed, and so the town house looked as if someone had died within. Mr. Markham was to stay in London to search for Mira or wait for her return.

Drusilla left them to it and went up to her room. She was all at once determined to do something, anything, to stay in London. She was sure the marquess was very like Mira. Therefore it followed that he was probably in love with her. But how to let him know?

With a courage and determination she had never known before, she changed out of her thin kid slippers and put on a pair of half boots, slung a cloak around her shoulders, and picked up her reticule. She walked boldly down the stairs. The drawing room was closed, and from behind it came the sound of voices as Mr. and Mrs. Markham bemoaned Mira's dreadful behavior and Charles commiserated with them. 'The carriage has not been ordered, Miss Markham,' said the butler.

'I am only going to walk around the square and take the air,' replied Drusilla, opening the door, not realizing that she had made two great breaks from the usual ordered pattern of her life already. Miss Drusilla Markham never dressed herself or opened a door when there was a servant to do it for her.

Ignoring the butler's protest that she was not accompanied by a maid and that he would call one of the footmen, Drusilla went out into the square and hurried off. Although she could easily have walked to Grosvenor Square, Drusilla, not used to walking anywhere, hailed a hack. For Drusilla to get into a London hack with an ancient driver leering on the box was as brave as any other female boarding a lugger full of villainous sailors. She wondered if she might faint from sheer excess of bravery.

But the hack creaked its smelly way to Grosvenor Square without incident.

Drusilla then paid off the driver, marched up the steps, and hammered on the door.

The marquess, on being informed that Miss Markham had called to see him, stared coldly at his butler and said, 'Without a maid?'

'Yes, my lord.'

'Oh, send her away! Is there no end to her folly?'

'May I say, my lord, that it is not Miss Mira Markham who has called but the elder, Miss Drusilla Markham. I do not have her card. The lady forgot her card case.'

The marquess felt a stab of anxiety. Something must have happened to Mira to bring the usually correct Drusilla to his town house.

'Tell her I will be with her directly,' he said.

Drusilla stood up as he entered and curtsied. 'You must forgive me, my lord,' she said, 'but only concern for my little sister would bring me here.'

'If you think Mira is here with me, then you are very much mistaken.'

'I know she is not.'

'Then why are you here?'

'May I be seated? I came in a hack.'

'What an adventure!' he said dryly. 'Please sit down. Some refreshment?'

'No, thank you, my lord. I have come to explain why Mira ran away.'

'That being?' he asked with seeming indifference.

'Well, it is all very odd to me. She says she is desperately in love with you, and she could not bear to be married to a man with whom she was so much in love knowing he did not return that love. And, of course, she does not like the idea of your being forced to marry her. She is very wild and impulsive . . .'

Drusilla's voice trailed away before the blaze of emotion in the marquess's eyes. 'Where has she gone?'

'Home, to the country. Such a mistake because I am to be taken out of London, and we are going to the country, too.'

'Thank you for telling me this, Miss Markham. I will go and fetch her.'

'She will not answer unless you tell her you are in love with her.' Drusilla looked at him doubtfully.

'Be assured, I shall tell her that.'

Drusilla rose gracefully to her feet. 'Then I shall tell Mama and Papa that the engagement is on again, and we can be comfortable. All this pulsing emotion seems most odd to me. It must be like having perpetual indigestion or disorder of the spleen, I think. Do warn Mira that an excess of emotion causes wrinkles.'

'I shall do that. Now, Miss Markham, I shall send you home in one of my carriages,'

'Too kind. It is dangerous for a lady of my delicacy to take more than one hack.'

*   *   *

Mr. and Mrs. Markham and Charles were still fretting about how to find Mira. Not one of them had even considered the idea that she had simply gone home to the country. When the door opened and Drusilla walked in, they looked at her in surprise, all taking in the fact that she was in her outdoor clothes.

'I took a hack,' said Drusilla proudly.

Mrs. Markham looked amazed. 'Why, what are you talking about?' Hope lit up her eyes. 'Do you know where Mira is? Did you go to see her?'

'Yes, I know where Mira is. But I went to see Grantley.'

'You *what*?' Mr. Markham turned red with amazement, shock, and anger. 'Is Mira with him? Did that scoundrel lie to me?'

'Mira is at home in the country. She left on the stage this morning. I went to tell Grantley that she had run away because she loved him.'

'Run away because she loved him? That does not make sense,' said Mrs. Markham. 'And how *could* you call at a gentleman's town house?'

'I was very courageous, was I not?' said Drusilla. 'But when I told him, he said he loved her as well, so he has gone to the country to bring her back. So we need not leave, and we can be comfortable again.'

'What is this farrago of nonsense?' demanded Charles sternly.

'It is not nonsense,' retorted Drusilla angrily. 'I have been most brave. Mira felt he was being forced to marry her. She said she could not bear to be married to a man with whom she was in love but who did not love her, and so he has gone to tell her he loves her as well.'

Mr. Markham took a deep breath. 'I would not have believed Grantley, at his age, to be capable of such mawkish thoughts.'

'Oh, I agree,' said Drusilla. 'But I am quite decided that he and Mira are very alike, so they should suit very well.'

'It sounds like a Haymarket play,' said Mr. Markham, 'but the family reputation is saved, for I was about to cancel the renewed notice of the engagement, and that would have caused even more fuss. I should be very angry with you, Drusilla, for not telling us in the first place where Mira had gone, but all has worked out very well.'

'I think you have done splendidly,' said Charles, his eyes now glowing with admiration.

And Drusilla agreed.

*　　　*　　　*

Mira was bored and lonely. Mr. and Mrs. George, the caretakers, had grumbled dreadfully at her arrival, and she had said she would attend to herself, correctly divining that their discontent was caused by the thought of any extra work.

Once she had removed her masculine clothes, she found she was reluctant to put them on again, feeling that if she had behaved more like a lady, then the marquess might not have been so indifferent to her.

And so she saddled up her mare, Sally, with

a sidesaddle, and wearing an old riding dress, she rode about the countryside to tire herself out and keep all the sad thoughts at bay.

On the second day she awoke to hear steady rain drumming on the roof. The house was cold and unfired. She rose, washed, and dressed, then wondered what to do to pass the day. She had avoided the townspeople, knowing that questions would be asked about why she had returned home alone. Mrs. Dunstable, her former mentor, was visiting relatives in the south, and so she was spared her attentions. But as the day wore on and she wandered around the cold rooms, the furniture still shrouded under holland covers, she found herself wishing that Mrs. Dunstable had been around. She thought constantly of the marquess, wondering what he was doing, if he ever thought of her, or if he considered he had had a lucky escape.

At last she could bear the inactivity no longer and changed into her riding dress, saddled her mare, and rode off over the soggy lawns and along the twisting path through the home woods, wondering how she could ever have fancied herself in love with Charles. The canopy of leaves stopped the worst of the downpour from reaching her.

She dismounted, left the mare to crop the scraggly wet patches of grass on either side of the path, and sat down on a fallen log under a tree.

How many innocent dreams she had had in these very woods. How childish they seemed now. She had sat on this very log and imagined walking and talking with Charles. And then, before going to London, she had imagined herself married to him.

Now it was the marquess who filled her thoughts. But he was far away in London, and he would never walk these woods with her. In fact, it was highly unlikely she would ever see him again. Her parents would certainly not waste money on another Season for one so disgraced. Life stretched out in front of her, years of loneliness and sadness.

A tear rolled down her cheek, mingling with the rainwater. She looked up at the branches above her head. They were not such a protection as she had first thought, and she was just realizing that if she sat there much longer, she was going to become very wet indeed when she heard someone approaching. The woods were very still. She could hear someone walking toward her, even though the ground was soft.

She started up, wondering who it could be. The Georges never went into the woods—in fact, she thought, they were too lazy to even leave the house.

When she saw the tall, mud-stained, and travel-weary Marquess of Grantley, she thought for one moment that her eyes were playing tricks on her. But he came right up to her and stood before her as real as the trees and the falling rain.

'Why are you here?' she asked weakly.

'Because I love you.'

She looked wildly around. 'I must be dreaming this.'

'No, darling idiot, and why did you not tell me you loved me?'

'How . . . how do you know?'

'You can thank the correct Drusilla for that. She not only called at my town house without a maid, mark you—but she came in a hack, which she considered to be in the same league as scaling the Alps.'

'Oh, dear,' said Mira, not knowing whether to laugh or cry. 'I can hardly believe it.'

'So, my beloved, are we going to stand here discussing the merits of Drusilla, or are you going to kiss me?'

'Rupert!' She threw herself into his arms. Her first kiss was wet and clumsy. But the second landed fair and square on his mouth with such passion that he clutched hold of her like a drowning man, returning passion with passion while the rain dripped on both of them and ran down their faces.

At last he put her from him and said shakily, 'I am deuced wet and tired. Let us return to the house and stir up that surly caretaker.'

They walked slowly back, Mira leading her horse. When she reached the house, she told him to go inside while she took her horse round to the stables and rubbed it down.

'Don't you have grooms?' he asked impatiently.

'Yes, of course, but I always see to my mare myself.'

When she returned from the stables, she could hear the marquess's voice raised in anger, demanding food and fires. As she walked in, Mr. George was saying defiantly, 'I was only hired to look after this-here place, not to run about making fires and cooking meals. Me and Mrs. George is leaving.'

'Then hurry up about it,' said the marquess, 'because I am sick of the sight of your face!'

'Now we are really in disgrace,' mourned Mira as she led him into the drawing room. 'No chaperons at all. You had best move to the nearest inn.'

'We are to be married, so people can think what they like. We shall begin by making ourselves comfortable. I will go to the stables and get one of the lads to bring piles of wood. Strip some of the chairs of their covers, my love, for it is like living in a mausoleum. As soon as we have a roaring fire here and in the bedchambers—if you will show me which one I may sleep in—then I will change, and we will both raid the kitchen, for I am sharp-set.'

Mr. George later said he felt cheated when he learned how the marquess had paid the small stable staff to fetch wood, light fires, and make the house comfortable. If his high-and-mighty lordship had said how he was prepared to pay, Mr. George became fond of moaning, then he and the missus would have stayed.

The marquess decided they should use not the drawing room but a small morning room on the ground floor as both drawing room and dining room. When they had changed out of their wet clothes, he asked Mira, 'Can you cook?'

'I am afraid I have not the slightest idea how to go on.'

'I think I can manage something,' he said. 'Let us repair to the kitchen and raid the larder.'

They decided instead of carrying a meal of cold ham, bread, and cheese up to the morning room to have it by the kitchen fire.

They dined side by side at the kitchen table, kissing and eating and then kissing again.

'We are behaving shamefully,' said Mira. 'I thought I was supposed to behave in a correct way.'

'You will—when we are married. We are having a little adventure.'

They fell then to talking, as lovers do, about when they had first fallen in love. 'I think I must have been in love with you all along,' said the marquess. 'But my pride would not let me realize it, particularly when you were drooling over your so-dear Charles.'

'"Drooling" is cruel, Rupert. I just had not

192

come to my senses.'

'So, now that you have come to your senses, kiss me again.'

He lifted her onto his knees and held her close. His hands caressed her breasts, and she felt dimly that it ought to be shocking instead of feeling like the most natural thing in the world.

At last he rose and lifted her in his arms, blew out the candles on the table, and by the light of the fire, made his way to the door.

He carried her all the way upstairs, kissing her repeatedly while the dark house seemed to reel about her.

When Mr. Markham was finally to return home, he questioned the stable staff. Had they or hadn't they?

But all the grooms and stable lads could do was shake their heads. How could they know? They were not indoor staff.

*   *   *

On their return to London the marquess took Mira first to meet his mother.

'I am pleased to meet you at last,' said the dowager marchioness, looking anything but as she gave Mira a limp handshake.

'You do understand,' said the marquess, 'that we are to be married?'

'I suppose so,' said his mother ungraciously. 'But you have caused a great deal of scandal.

First an engagement was announced—without your even telling me about it—and then it was canceled, and then it was on again. People kept asking me questions and questions, and I had to admit I did not know what my only son was doing.'

'I am sorry for that, Mother, but as you can see, you will be dancing at our wedding.'

The dowager marchioness's eyes brightened. 'A wedding, of course. Mrs. Anderson, bring me my notebook. I must make lists. Perhaps in a year's time, or is that too soon?'

'Too late. I am getting a special license today, and we will be married quietly in a fortnight's time.'

'Merciful heavens! More scandal!' Her old eyes raked up and down Mira's slim figure. 'I assume there is good reason for the haste.'

'Every reason. We are in love.'

His mother looked bewildered. 'Love? At your age, Rupert?'

'Yes, Mother. Love.'

The dowager marchioness suddenly lost her temper. 'I have prayed that you would meet some beautiful and graceful lady. But you have chosen this . . . I am sorry, my dear. But you are just not suitable to be the Marchioness of Grantley.'

The marquess stood up and held out his hand to Mira. 'Come, my dear. Mother, I will let you know when and where the wedding is to

194

be held. Whether you come or not is your affair. But you must never, ever again insult Mira the way you have done now.'

When they had left, the dowager marchioness began to cry. Mrs. Anderson handed her smelling salts and a handkerchief and waited until the old lady was somewhat more composed before saying quietly, 'You must not distress yourself. It will all work out very well. Mira Markham is very young but generous in spirit. If you handle it well, you can be a constant visitor to their home. If you continue to be rude to her, you will not be welcome.'

'And why should I want to have anything to do with her?'

'You will want to see your grandchildren,' said Mrs. Anderson firmly. 'That young lady is going to have lots of babies. You have always prayed for grandchildren, or so you told me. And now you do not want to have anything to do with a courageous and kind young lady who is going to give them to you.'

The dowager marchioness dried her eyes. 'I never thought of that,' she said weakly.

'Your son, Lord Grantley, is very much in love. If you have given Miss Mira a disgust of you, you may end up estranged from him. I suggest you call on Miss Mira as soon as possible and make your amends.'

And so Mrs. Anderson went on in her gentle way, urging and manipulating until the poor dowager marchioness was thoroughly frightened by the thought that her son might not come near her again.

When she finally called for her carriage to go to the Markhams, Mrs. Anderson heaved a sigh of relief. She felt she owed Mira a great deal. Had she not been inspired by the girl's courage, then she would still be trapped with Lady Jansen.

*　　　*　　　*

Lady Jansen was staying at an inn at Dover, waiting for a favorable wind to bear her over to France. There were many other English tourists waiting to embark as well. The end of hostilities with France had sent many English flocking to the ports. Paris was still the mecca of fashion, and that was where Lady Jansen was bound.

She no longer longed for the marquess. On the contrary, she hated him. She was convinced now that he had led her on disgracefully only to spurn her. She knew she would have to stay away for some time before London society forgave her. Mrs. Gardener, that arch gossip, had been the worst. Because what had fascinated Mrs. Gardener most about Lady Jansen's story was not the scandalous behavior of Mira Markham but the scandalous behavior of Lady Jansen, who could go to such extremes out of 'spite and jealousy.'

Lady Jansen had seen Mrs. Gardener in Pall Mall just before she left, and Mrs. Gardener had cut her dead.

She went out for a walk to cool her angry thoughts, looking at the masts of the ships in the harbor dancing crazily in the wind like some kind of mad forest.

She was just about to turn back when she saw a familiar face, lit by a riding light hanging from the bowsprit of a schooner. Mr. Diggs!

She marched up to him and confronted him. 'Traitor!' she growled.

'Oh, it is you, my lady,' he said mildly.

'I will call for the constable and have you arrested,' raged Lady Jansen. 'I will get my money back.'

'As you will,' said Mr. Diggs indifferently. 'But what will you tell him, and what proof do you have? The story of your malice is only gossip at the moment, but the minute you call the constable, it will reach the newspapers and be there in black and white for the whole country to read.'

She stared at him in baffled fury. He touched his hat and walked away from her along the waterfront until the darkness swallowed him up. She was never to see him again.

*   *   *

The marriage of the Marquess of Grantley was

a small but elegant affair. Church weddings were not fashionable, but predictably the couple had therefore decided to have a church wedding. Only close members of the family had been invited, but society crowded outside St. George's, Hanover Square, to get a look at this pair who had caused so much gossip. Because of the speed of the wedding, bets were being laid at White's as to whether the bride was already pregnant or not, a fact that the marquess had wisely kept from Mira.

The ceremony was moving because of the couple's obvious love for each other. Mrs. Anderson wept quietly all the way through it, but the dowager marchioness was dry-eyed. She had done very well by affecting to be delighted with Mira, but she still thought her son was making a disastrous mistake. Mrs. Markham was weeping with sheer relief. She had lived in dread every day right up to the wedding that the fiery Mira would suddenly tell her the whole thing was off.

Mira was small and dainty in white Brussels lace and for once did not feel at all sad about or jealous of the admiration her beautiful sister was receiving as bridesmaid.

The wedding breakfast, held at the dowager marchioness's, was accounted a pleasant affair, and then the guests crowded outside to wave good-bye to the married couple.

Charles took Drusilla's hand in his and heaved a sigh. 'How much in love they are!